PRAISE F

You are living y
and family. Your farm is a ...,
Americana where generations before you claimed
their livelihood; you are proud of what you do and all
is well, until there's a knock at your door. An
attorney and a handful of local, criminal
politicians try to force the sale of your property. They
have everything to gain; you have everything to lose.
The fight begins and the pages turn. This is an
excellent literary novel which will propel the reader
into becoming a cheerleader for the good guy.

Virginia Young, Author,
I Call Your Name and other novels

Adelene Ellenberg's legal thriller *Eminent Crimes* is
absorbing...entertaining...chilling and inspirational
all at once...There are heroes and villains...each of
them is a well-defined and fully-fleshed character.
Eminent Crimes takes a frank look at the abuses
made possible by an ill-considered Supreme Court
decision and outlines the challenges aggrieved
plaintiffs face when fighting to retain their property;
and it's presented in an exciting and fast-paced
thriller. *Eminent Crimes* is highly recommended.

Jack Magnus for Readers' Favorite

...a highly captivating legal and political thriller. The
novel exposes how deep corruption runs in public
office and the massive abuse of power that the
elected leaders practice in a bid to fill their own
pockets, with no regard to the way their decisions
affect the common man. It is a very gripping story
and all the characters are special and compelling...a
one of a kind story...

Faridah Nassozi for Readers' Favorite

MORE PRAISE FOR
EMINENT CRIMES

Adelene Ellenberg writes a sensational legal thriller in *Eminent Crimes*…an outstanding, heart-throbbing crime novel. The story baits you with a great narrative hook, and then pulls you into its dynamic plot scheme. Adelene Ellenberg's political tale is full of action and vivid descriptions. She paints a captivating story, and brings it to life with waves of emotion. *Eminent Crimes* depicts the controversy of "eminent domain" by revealing the greed of the lofty over the individual land owner. Does the good of the many outweigh the good of the few or the one? At what cost or measure? And who has the right or power to decide? This is the conflict that propels the action of the characters. The cast of characters are written with depth and intensity, all arcing with precision at the climax. The protagonist's strength of character to rise up and defend, versus the antagonist's willingness to stoop to the depths of criminal corruption to take, make it a fast paced, can't put it down, enthralling read. As the action begins to fall, hold on! It isn't over yet. A few more surprises await you. Ellenberg keeps the reader engaged until the very end.

Cheryl E. Rodriguez for Readers' Favorite

Eminent Crimes by Adelene Ellenberg is a lovely book…If you're looking for a light-hearted mystery, then *Eminent Crimes: A Legal Thriller* will catch your attention from the beginning.

Michelle Stanley for Readers' Favorite

*Dear Miriam
& Louie—
Good luck in all your
future endeavors!*

EMINENT CRIMES

A Legal Thriller

Adelene Ellenberg (signature)

Adelene Ellenberg

Riverhaven Books

www.RiverhavenBooks.com

Eminent Crimes is a work of fiction. While some of the settings are actual, any similarity regarding names, characters, or incidents is entirely coincidental. Any errors in the law are entirely the author's.

Copyright© 2014 by Adelene Ellenberg
Revised and reprinted 2015

Published in the United States
by Riverhaven Books,
www.RiverhavenBooks.com

ISBN: 978-1-937588-39-7

Printed in the United States of America
by Country Press, Lakeville, Massachusetts
Edited and designed by
Stephanie Lynn Blackman
Whitman, Massachusetts

*I would like to thank the following people who
helped me in so many ways:*

*Joyce Quimby and the late Fran Shonio,
who founded Talespinners, bringing together a
community of like-minded people;*

*my fellow writers
Nancy E. Gay, Phyllis Goldfeder,
Christine Muratore, Rosalie Bingham,
Kathy Golden, Joan Davenport,
Joanne Temperly, Virginia Deknis,
Sheryl Amaral, Sandy Churchill,
the late Judy Northrup,
and the late Jean McFayden;*

*my two readers,
Dee McNamara and Lynne Cole Anderson,
for their trustworthy opinions and suggestions;*

*Sandra Gardner at CrimeBake,
who channeled the title I turned out to need;*

*and last, but not least, my dedicated editor
who made it all happen:
Stephanie Blackman at Riverhaven Books.*

*Dedicated to my three
sweethearts,
DALE, ROBERT, and STACY,
with my love and gratitude*

CHAPTER 1

From the barn door shadows, he stared at the approaching car with rising dread. The silver Cadillac crunched onto his gravel driveway, its arrogant nose swinging wide. The car stopped, the engine cut off. Two men emerged, straightening their suit sleeves. Robert Jaston recognized them from town. The hunched stance of the taller man and the jaunty air of the shorter told all he needed to know.

He watched as they stood still too long, seeming to inventory his assets: his farmhouse, his barn, his outbuildings, his herd of well-fed black and white Holsteins grazing contentedly on lush, green fields. As they scanned the grounds for someone to talk to, Robert ducked a little deeper into the barn shadows.

Seeing no one, the arrivals headed for farmhouse's closest door.

Robert Jaston's thoughts flashed to his wife, Maureen, their ten-year-old twin daughters, Layla and Shaina, and their teenaged son, Jacob, who were in the house, unaware of strangers approaching. A sense of urgency overtook him, and he started towards their farmhouse, picking up speed as he went.

The two men stood at the farmhouse's granite doorstep and rang the doorbell. Maureen opened the door and greeted them with a smile.

Don't let them in, he thought as he dashed across the last length. *I don't like the way they were looking over my land and farm. They're up to no good.*

Maureen opened the door wide and the two men stepped inside.

Dammit! My wife is nice to everyone, he thought. *It's her chief fault.* Robert leapt onto the granite doorstep just as the screen door was about to shut, shoved open the door, and stepped into the kitchen. He stood there, lightly panting, sweat beading on his sun-burned skin. His dark, shaggy, flyblown hair stuck out of his baseball cap. He hadn't shaved that morning, giving him a lean, hungry appearance. He stared intently at the two well-groomed men.

"Robert," said Maureen, breaking the awkward silence. "I'm glad you're here. As you can see, we've got visitors. They've got some sort of business to talk over with us."

The two men had already taken chairs at the round, wooden kitchen table. Both men rose and tried to shake his hand. Robert Jaston ignored them. He turned to face Maureen. "Do you know who these two guys are?"

Maureen was taken aback at his uncharacteristic lack of manners. "Umm, no. Should I?"

Robert gestured to the taller, stooped man who sat tentatively on the edge of his chair, as if he didn't quite belong there. "That's Attorney Tobias Meachum, the lawyer with all the right political connections. You must've heard about his father, the judge, back when you moved to town..."

"Leave my father out of this," the lawyer softly growled.

"His daddy was known as 'Judge-Buy-Me-Off-Meachum' to all the local criminals who would cut a deal," Robert continued, forcefully. No longer able to ignore the sweat that had sprung out at his temples from his sprint across the yard, he reached for his handkerchief in his overalls and mopped his brow, then plopped into a kitchen chair. It creaked ferociously.

"All lies," muttered the lawyer.

Maureen turned to look sharply at Tobias Meachum. "I remember now. Your father let that drunk guy off after he had killed that little boy on the bike. That was years ago, but I still remember it because the boy lived down the street from me." She frowned and turned quickly to the other man. "And who are you?"

A white smile blazed in a handsome face. "I'm Michael Quinn. I'm the local 'go-to' guy."

"Otherwise known as Mickey Quinn," interjected Robert. "He's known to make people's problems go away."

Maureen eyed Quinn curiously. He was an enigma: his sky-blue eyes were unblinkingly earnest, his blond hair fell casually over his forehead, his voice lilted like a finely-tuned violin. He was undeniably charming, despite any misgivings she might have.

"Oh, yes. I should have recognized you from our open town meetings," she said. "You've certainly run them like your personal fiefdom."

"I see my reputation precedes me," said Mickey Quinn smugly.

"Your reputation is that you're a little too slick for your own good," Maureen said.

"Now, now...mustn't judge me so harshly...you don't even know what I'm going to say yet."

"That's true."

"So you're willing to hear me out?"

3

"I guess so," said Maureen.

Robert expelled a lengthy sigh.

"Coffee'd be appreciated, if you have it, Mrs. Jaston," said the lawyer.

"Alright, gentlemen. Let it never be said that a Jaston has failed to show proper hospitality. I'll put on a new pot right now."

Robert and the two visitors watched silently as Maureen filled the empty coffeepot with cold water, then wiped her hands on the backside of her jeans. She turned to the coffeemaker and filled it with their best coffee, the stuff they normally used for Sunday mornings.

Did these two think she was running a restaurant? Robert thought sourly.

The sounds and smells of percolating coffee filled the kitchen as Maureen organized the cups, saucers, spoons, sugar, and cream.

These two don't deserve any effort on your part, Robert silently told his wife, wishing he had the nerve to say it out loud.

Once she was satisfied with her preparations, she sat. "So, what's this all about?"

"Mr. Jaston, Mrs. Jaston," said Quinn, "you have a fine dairy farm here."

"Thank you," Maureen replied. "But you didn't come here to just give us compliments."

Quinn ignored the sarcasm and leaned forward to speak in a low, confidential tone. "Have you two ever thought of doing anything else, besides farming?" said Quinn, his blue eyes moist with soulful empathy.

4

"Of course not," said Robert. "We're very happy here." He lifted his chin and waited.

Maureen proudly stated, "Robert was raised here. He's been on this farm his whole life." She firmly brushed some of her long copper-colored hair behind her shoulder. A shaft of sunlight angled into the kitchen and made it shine.

The color of my treasure, thought Robert.

Noticing the coffee was brewed, she stood up to fetch the pot. She looked at her husband, wondering at his curious reticence. She began pouring cups of coffee. The three men waited until she was finished to say anything more.

Quinn fingered his green silk tie. The lulling voice was even gentler now. "Have you two ever thought of selling your property?"

Robert and Maureen looked across the table at one another. Maureen's gray-blue eyes were clear as river water; Robert's were black, gleaming, and opaque as oil. They each knew what the other was thinking by a mere glance. Maureen smiled slightly to comfort Robert, and he felt her reassurance, her steadiness.

Robert turned back to Quinn and Meachum. "Let's get down to brass tacks: what's this all about?"

Now the lawyer leaned forward. "The town of Longbottom needs your property for a very important project. So does the Commonwealth of Massachusetts."

Robert felt his blood surge behind his eyes and adrenaline flood his extremities. His heart pounded. Making a fist on his right knee, he knew this was going to be the fight of his life. Despite an effort to keep his voice even, it came out in a strangled cry: "I *won't* sell!"

"A big company is coming to Longbottom; that would bring lots of money and jobs," Quinn continued as if nothing had just been said.

"I *can't* sell," Robert said more to himself than to anyone else. He began to look around the kitchen as if seeing it for the first time: the wide, honey-colored pine floors which slanted towards the south-facing wall; the oval braided rug in front of the sink; the horsehair and plaster walls; the wide, wooden beams in the low ceiling; the rack of iron skillets; the twins' artwork stuck on the refrigerator with magnets; the homemade muffins cooling on the rack.

Robert took off his Red Sox cap and raked his callused fingers through his thick black hair until it stood on end. His gaze came back into focus on the two men. Regaining his composure he asked, "What does Longbottom need *my* land for?"

"We told you. A big company," said Quinn.

"What kind of company?"

Quinn and Meachum exchanged a glance.

"A casino," said Quinn.

"A casino?" repeated Robert, rolling his eyes. "Wonderful! Introducing gambling to Longbottom. That's just what this town needs."

"Longbottom people will have first dibs at the jobs. We take care of our own," said Quinn, suddenly pious-sounding. "Plus it'll bring in hotels and restaurants to the area."

Robert Jaston leaned back hard in his chair, a look of disgust on his face. He turned his head to stare out the window at his barn, his outbuildings, his herd of dairy cows grazing. The thought of his land bulldozed beyond recognition, paved over, ghastly concrete buildings standing where his grove of apple trees now stood made him shudder.

The conversation had skittered to a halt.

"We're businessmen, Mr. Jaston, and we've come to buy your farm." Quinn grinned broadly, trying to make eye contact with both Robert and Maureen who ignored his efforts. "Aren't you even a little bit curious as to how much money you'd get?"

"That'd be the first thing I'd want to know," Tobias added.

"You'd send your own grandmother into servitude if it'd make you a tidy sum," said Robert, fixing his eyes on Quinn.

"I guess you believe ignorance is bliss."

Robert's mouth tightened. "That's right."

"Well, then. I'll just lay it on you: eight million for your one hundred acres."

"Doesn't matter," Robert said. "Selling—selling out, is just plain wrong! The money, while it might be a temptation to some, won't take the place of what we have here."

Quinn watched Maureen covertly, looking for a chink in the Jaston armor. She was unreadable, so he pushed on. "Think of the life you'd have. You could retire on easy street. No more back-breaking work, day in, day out." Still, he didn't get any reaction. "Think of Jacob, Layla, and Shaina: you could send all three of them to college. With that kind of money, they'd be set for life."

At the mention of her children's names, Maureen's head swung towards Quinn. "You're an absolute fiend! Robert's family has been on this land since his great-grandfather started this farm in 1892. This farm is our children's legacy."

"It's all a matter of how you look at it," said Quinn, aiming his charmer-smile at Maureen. "This could be a new legacy."

The four of them stared at one another, the silence becoming increasingly awkward.

Tobias Meachum finally spoke. "You do know, Mrs. Jaston, that there are other ways to get your land."

"Is that a threat, sir?" Maureen decided her hospitality had ended. She started to gather the cups of coffee, still half-filled, from in front of the two men and took them to the sink.

Slightly taken aback, Tobias continued, "I wouldn't call it a threat; it's a fact."

Quinn added, "Your farm is the last large parcel of land left in the area. Longbottom has been chosen due to its proximity to highways and the train station. This casino is going to happen. It will be easier for your entire family if you just accept our generous offer."

"You two are really something else," said Maureen. "You come here expecting us to welcome you as you tell us we'll be giving up our livelihood, our home, and our way of life. Are you nuts?"

"As I said before, it's all a matter of how you look at it, my dear," said Quinn. "Maybe the thought of eight million dollars will grow on you."

Robert pounded his fist on the wooden table. "I already said, I'm not selling this farm, period. And especially not to make way for a damned casino."

"Ah, my stubborn farmer-friend, there are ways for us to take possession," said Mickey Quinn. "Just ask my lawyer friend here about that. Remember: you can't stop progress."

"You're no longer welcome in my house." Robert stood firmly. Through gritted teeth he said, "Get out. Now!"

Mickey Quinn and Tobias Meachum exchanged vexed looks, rose, then departed. As they walked down the gravel driveway, the Jastons watched the two intruders get into the silver Cadillac. The vehicle made an irritatingly slow five-point turn before finally leaving.

Maureen approached her husband and took his hand. He gave it a reassuring squeeze and firmly stated, "If those two think they can take our home from us, it'll be *over my dead body*!"

CHAPTER 2

Every muscle ached and every joint crackled in Denton
Clay's body since the night of the car accident. He
hadn't slept in over a week. He dreamt of a deer's head
rising up from the street with a yawning mouth, opening
to his windshield, roaring with rage, which rose in pitch
until it became the scream of a human girl. The deer's
head transformed into a screaming girl's face glued to
his windshield. He kept swerving from side to side to
dislodge the face from the glass, but it was stuck. There
was no escape. This was when he woke up each night,
drenched in sweat, with the bed sheets tangled around
his legs like a mummy's wrappings.

These days he ran on nervous energy. He couldn't
swallow food. It all became thick and impenetrable in
his throat, like trying to swallow a washcloth whole. He
relied on cup after cup of coffee to quell his hunger.

His imagination became ever more feverish. He
suspected gossip circulating amongst the bank personnel
about the car accident. Yesterday, when he had swerved
around a corner towards the coffee-station, he heard one
bank employee tell another that it was the governor's
niece who was hit. He silently prayed that it had nothing
to do with his accident. If it did, he was in deep trouble.
He hoped it had been a different accident. Thank God no
one had been around to see his expression when he
heard that tidbit. He had scuttled back to his office
without any coffee despite a biting hunger.

Denton Clay was beginning to regret what he had done immediately following the accident. He knew he had had too many gin and tonics to pass any kind of breathalyzer tests, so he had left the scene of the accident. No one had been around. It had been a drizzly night, with a silver haze around the few streetlights on the town common. At the time, he had genuinely thought he had hit a deer.

It wasn't until the next morning, when he got up with a blinding hangover under a blazing sun, that he saw the damage to his Lexus. His car was parked the driveway of his townhouse, nose in, so, fortunately, the neighbors couldn't see. That was when he noticed the huge dent in the front bumper and hood of his car. Then, even worse, he saw the piece of fabric from a raincoat and a bloody hunk of long, brown hair attached to the edge of the fender. He had almost puked at the sight. Then he had panicked.

In his terror, he had called Mickey Quinn. Thinking back, he winced to remember that his voice had shaken during that conversation. He remembered babbling something to the effect that there was no way he could face the public humiliation of an arrest, a trial, a conviction, and, Heaven forbid, going to prison. Something had to be done, and discreetly.

Mickey had been as soothing as another tall gin and tonic at that moment. Denton had felt an icy calm begin to soak his fevered brain as he strove to listen and comprehend just what Mickey was saying to him at that moment. Something about keeping his car out of sight until one of his guys came around with a tow truck to

11

get it. A shop would fix it, no questions asked. It'd cost him a pretty penny though.

No, he had no problem with the plan, none at all. And, yes, he'd of course be happy to help Mr. Michael Quinn in the future in any way he could.

Of course.

It's just that Denton Clay worked at Longbottom Savings Bank, and a Mr. Michael Quinn had been calling him at the bank, asking for him personally. Denton had been ever so carefully avoiding the phone calls, but it was becoming obvious he was doing so. He dared not avoid them any longer. He decided to retreat to the privacy of his office, where any conversation could take place behind a closed door. He was perversely proud that he had been able to keep up appearances despite everything. His folders were neatly stacked. His pens were in their cobalt jar, his stapler lined up too. He kept his air-conditioning a goose-flesh-raising cold, the better to maintain his temperament at a necessary cool.

The telephone at his desk buzzed. "A Mr. Quinn on line three," said the operator.

Denton took a deep breath. "Hello?"

"Denton! My man, how are ya?"

"I'm okay, I guess."

"How they hangin'?"

"By a thread, to be honest."

"Aww, come on. It ain't as bad as that!"

"Not much better. Been having a bit of indigestion."

"Stay off the blues-juice."

"I guess."

"My medical advice is free. Take what you can get. Whad d'ya say? Meantime, I got something for ya, Denton. An assignment."

"What?"

"All in good time. Stop by Quinn's Pub and Grill after work. I'll buy you a fruit drink. It'll be good for your liver."

"Just what I need: a cure by Mickey Quinn."

"Hey! The 'Mickey Quinn' is only for close personal associates. Michael Quinn to you, bub!"

"You're absolutely right, Mr. Quinn. My mistake."

"Just pullin' your string. See you later today."

"Sure."

And he had gone. What could he have done? Mickey Quinn had him by his small, shriveled ones. That was when Denton decided to tell his bank manager that he was feeling sick and needed to go home early, despite being the middle of summer when absolutely no one had the flu or a virus.

The summer sun was egg-yolk orange in a white sky, which made Denton lightheaded and nauseous. He got into his rental car, shuddering as he remembered how one co-worker had questioned him about where his Lexus was. He had pleaded engine trouble.

To head to Quinn's Pub and Grill, he had to go around that accursed town common, the scene of his accident. The smell of engine exhaust from traffic filtered through the air-conditioning vents. *When had this little country town become so busy?* A perpetual stream of traffic ran around the town common, which was a little-used oasis of green grass and brave trees. The stone monuments to the worthy dead were not affected by the roar of engines all around, but the living had been effectively chased away, but for the lone pedestrian who bucked the tide. Really, it was an affront to calm, serenity, and sanity.

When he pulled into the parking lot of Quinn's Pub and Grill, he noticed it was almost full. *Don't people work?* he wondered. He walked slowly in the heat and pulled open the massive wooden door.

It took a few moments for his eyes to adjust to the shadows, even though it was only mid-afternoon. He noticed that there were no windows. The lighting came from neon beer signs and the illumination around the bar. He looked around for Mickey Quinn and spotted him sitting in a corner booth on the left side. Denton realized that Mickey sat where he could watch the door and had already seen him. Denton put on the smile he wore to greet bank customers.

"Hey, Denton. Have a seat," Mickey waved his arm vaguely. "This is Tobias Meachum, a lawyer friend of mine. Do you two know each other?"

Denton and Toby made acknowledgement noises in unison. "Mr. Meachum does some work for the bank," said Denton.

"That's right," sniffed Toby, who then wiped his nose with the back of his hand.

Mickey rolled his eyes and handed him a napkin. "What would you like to drink, Denton?"

"A cranberry juice."

"I was kidding about the fruit juice." Mickey eyed

14

Denton quizzically, not sure if he was up to the job at hand. Denton was a slight fellow who looked elfin, with silver hair that stood on end around his head: a classic Albert Einstein haircut if there ever was one. He stood on his dignity a bit too much to harbor a sense of humor. Ah, well.

"Make that a ginger ale. Better for the digestion."

"Sure thing." Mickey signaled a waitress to come over to take their order.

They waited until she had left for conversation to resume.

"Good. I'll make everything brief. Toby and I are interested in getting ahold of some land in town. We think you can help."

"Oh?"

"Do you know the Jaston farm?"

"Of course."

"That's the land."

"Do the Jastons want to sell?"

"No." Mickey grinned widely. "But I never let a little thing like the word 'no' get in my way."

Denton sighed and waited.

"You're a banker, right?"

"I have that privilege." He straightened his slender back.

"Well, today's your lucky day. You'll get to be the ultimate banker who forecloses on their land."

Denton spoke carefully. "The bank won't foreclose on them without reason."

"There's always a reason: some condition of the loan hasn't been met, some small item to legally hang your hat on, as my friend Toby says so eloquently."

"I can't think of any special conditions in the Jaston loan."

"Find one. Anything. Anything will do. Just do it. Need I say more?"

***

It was the talk of the town. It was the talk of the Commonwealth of Massachusetts. It was the talk on all the news stations located in Boston. Just who had killed the niece of the governor in a hit-and-run accident? The identity of the perpetrator was a mystery, and the news reporters from Boston came swarming out of the city to descend upon tiny town of Longbottom.

First, the news cameras took footage of the picturesque town common and the country stores surrounding it. Then the reporters began stopping townspeople on the sidewalk to ask them their opinions. Of course nobody had any idea who had done it, so the reporters came up dry. The Longbottom police chief was interviewed, and he was adamant that every possible lead would be chased down to the fullest extent. Then the governor himself was interviewed on television, moist-eyed, vowing that he would not rest until justice was done for his sister's youngest daughter, his baby niece, Amanda.

Her name had to be Amanda, Denton thought.

During the barrage of reporters, he felt as if the word "Killer" was painted in scarlet on his forehead. He knew the word was invisible to the world, but he felt as if a person with second sight would see it and call him out. He felt vulnerable, as if he would inevitably encounter that one person and be arrested on the spot. It was all he could do to not turn himself in and make a full confession, and thereby be done with all the suspense. But then he would think of the ensuing trial, and he would bite his lips once more.

After three days in Longbottom, the Boston reporters had gleaned every shred of information they could. It was time to move on. The camera trucks rolled up their equipment and drove over to the highway that headed back to Boston.

Denton Clay breathed a sigh of relief now that the reporters were gone, but he knew that his troubles were not over. Mickey Quinn could turn him in at any time, and he'd be a dead duck. He had embarked upon a course of action that involved subterfuge and deception, and it was too late to turn back now. The damage was done and irreparable, and he had to live with the consequences.

CHAPTER 3

Mickey left his pub at 2:00 a.m., after the receipts had
been counted and locked in the safe. He drove on the
center of the street, like he owned it, straddling the
dividing line. He liked to avoid potholes, which tended
to line the edges of roads. Besides, no one else was out
at that hour other than the town cops at the donut shop,
and they all knew him. Meanwhile, he figured he'd see
the lights of an oncoming car in time to avoid a crash. If
not, Clarisse would be a sad woman.

At least he hoped she would be. *You never know the
secret heart of a woman*, he thought. He wondered again
whether Clarisse really loved him or whether she had
just married him for his money and his name. After all,
she was fifteen years younger. He smiled to himself: no
doubt he had robbed the cradle with Clarisse. At least
he'd always had foxy women.

Clarisse was his third wife, following Bridget, who
followed Annette. It occurred to him that his wives'
names were in alphabetical order. Ridiculous really. His
next wife, if it ever came to that, would have to be a
Donna or a Diane. He laughed out loud.

Well, if he died in a car crash, Clarisse and his exes
would all be outta luck, he thought. No children from
any of 'em, and none of them deserved to be a rich
widow. None of 'em had helped build up the family
business or brought any assets to the marriages. He had
willed his pub and all his other worldly goods to his best

friend, Tobias Meachum. Toby had been the only one in town who had stuck by him when things had turned grim. No need to dwell on all that now he reminded himself.

When he approached his house, he saw that all the lights were off, except the lone kitchen light in back that shone through the shutters. He parked in his oversized two-car garage and shut off the engine of his silver Cadillac. He listened to the engine ticking as it cooled and wondered if Clarisse was awake in the dark.

As he went inside he stood perfectly still to listen to the house sounds. Distantly, he heard disjointed laughter coming from a television. Clarisse was waiting up for him. He smiled to himself. *Good.*

"Hey, honey," he called upstairs.

"Hi, Mickey," Clarisse called down. "How was your night?"

He tromped up the bare, wooden stairs. "Busy." He appeared in the doorway of their large bedroom, which was completely dark but for the flickering gray light of the television.

"Did you eat? I could fix you something..."

"I ate...I ate..." He walked in alongside the king-sized bed and began unbuttoning his shirt, which he dropped on the floor. Then he unfastened his belt and let his pants slip down around his ankles. He kicked them off. "I'm hungry for something a little sweeter..."

"Honey?"

"You're my honeybuns, alright!" He bent over her body and reached down to give her breasts a squeeze through her nightgown. Then he pulled her upright and drew her to him tightly so they were pressed together, head to groin.

"Sweetie?"

"Time to stir the honey pot!"

"Mickey, I've got something to tell you…"

"What?"

"I got my period today."

"Aw, shit."

"I'm sorry, sweetie. You know I can't help it."

"Damn."

"Yeah, I hate it, too."

"So you're definitely not pregnant?"

"No."

"That's a damn shame." He turned away from her to sit on the edge of the bed. He leaned forward and planted his head heavily in his upturned hands. "How long's it been, now?"

"A year, year 'n a half, I'd say," said Clarisse.

"I'd say three."

"Who's counting?"

"Me," said Mickey Quinn.

"Why?'

"Because I'm forty-six. Gonna be fifty soon. Time to have a kid."

"I thought it was women who had biological clocks."

"Ha, ha."

"We should get tested," said Clarisse.

"I'm not going to any damn clinic to get tested!"

"Why not?"

"'Cause I know it's not me."

"How do you know?" asked Clarisse softly.

"Believe me: I know." He jerked his chin towards her emphatically and gave a sardonic grin.

"Oh, yeah?"

"I got a girl pregnant once, okay?"

"Oh?"

"She had a miscarriage. So she said."

"Oh."

"So, as you can see, it's not me."

"Mmmmm."

"You doubt me?"

"I don't know. Are you sure she was really pregnant? Was she trying to force you into a hasty marriage? Something doesn't add up."

"Like what?"

"Like how old were you and the girl when she got pregnant?"

"We were seniors in high school."

"Tell me more..."

"What?"

"Was she the town slut? Did she just want to get out of her parents' house real bad?"

Mickey Quinn licked his lips. "Yeah, the second thing. Her old man useta beat her something fierce."

"Figures."

"Why do you say that?"

"She probably saw getting pregnant and then married to you as her ticket out of her parents' house forever. How'd she miscarry?"

Mickey unclenched his fists and cupped his knees with his hands. He was silent, staring at the carpet in the flickering, gray light of the television. "Her old man beat the baby outta her. I wanted to go to their house and kill him, but my friend Toby stopped me from making the mistake of a lifetime."

Gently, Clarisse said, "How do you know for certain you were the father?"

Mickey was silent for a long time, still staring at the carpet. He sighed mournfully. "I guess I'll never know for certain, will I? Maybe she never knew, either."

"Why do you say that?"

"'Cause she was two-timing me with a football player named Munchkin."

"Munchkin?"

"Yeah. Munchkin was the nickname of this behemoth guy who played linebacker."

"Oh."

"And we were both doin' her. But I think I was the one who got her knocked up 'cause Munchkin claimed he always used protection."

Clarisse reached for his hand and clasped it. The two of them sat, watching a repetitive infomercial. Neither made a move to shut off the TV.

"So whaddya say, Mickey? Think we should be tested?"

"Not just yet, babe. I gotta settle my thoughts about all this."

CHAPTER 4

Denton nervously licked his lips and ran his slender fingers through his stand-up tufts of white hair. The effect was to make his hair look wilder, more Albert Einstein-like than ever. His co-workers at the bank joked that they could ascertain his mood by the condition of his hair. Today, he was running on frantic.

This wasn't going to be easy, he reflected. He took a deep breath, held it, and dialed Mickey Quinn's cell phone number. As it began to ring, he slowly exhaled.

"What's up, my man?" answered Mickey.

"I have an idea," he said in a thin voice.

"Shoot."

"I've gone over the terms of the Jaston loan, again and again, and there's simply no way to get the bank to foreclose on their loan. There just isn't. They're impeccable in their payments. They're never even late, much less miss a payment. It's impossible to fault them."

"So?"

"So the only kind of foreclosure that can happen is for nonpayment of taxes."

"You want Longbottom to be the bad guy, huh?" Mickey chuckled.

Denton ignored his laughter and went on. "The Jastons pay for their taxes with each loan payment, which is held in escrow until the time of payment. If the bank failed to pay their taxes, the town could initiate a foreclosure or a tax sale."

"And how would the bank not pay their taxes?"

"I don't know yet. I'm working on that. Maybe something in the bank's computer record. You know, a glitch."

"If you think you can do it."

"Maybe. I'm not sure."

"Say you can. When would this happen?"

"The next tax payment is due in November, and the one after that is due in May. There has to be a minimum of two missed tax payments for the town to start a tax sale."

"So you're saying the legal proceedings won't happen for at least a year?"

"Yeah, it'll take about that long, or longer. Actually, a lot longer, technically."

There was silence on the other end of the phone. Mickey Quinn sighed loudly. "Can't you speed matters up at all?"

"No, sir. Anyway, how soon do you need it to happen?"

"Sooner than a year from now."

Denton waited, hoping.

"You're disappointing me, Denton. Bigtime. Not-so-nice things happen when I'm unhappy."

"I've heard that."

"Then you know."

"Yes."

"So figure it out."

"I'll try, sir. I will." His voice rose to a whine. "But I don't know if I can."

"If you can't, then I can't. Know what I mean?"

"Yes," whispered Denton.

"Okay then. I'll be watching and waiting. We'll see, won't we?"

"I guess so."

"Time will tell," said Mickey Quinn as he hung up.

Putting down the phone, Denton realized he was shaking, physically. He sat rigidly in his desk chair, pondering the conversation that had just taken place. Did Mickey Quinn mean that he would tell on him, with that 'time will tell' crack? He tugged at his white hair harder, causing it to stand out from his head even more wildly. He realized that his fate hung in the balance. Everything depended on whether Mickey Quinn deemed him useful or not, and who could tell how matters would play out?

CHAPTER 5

Mickey rose from his couch to answer his doorbell on a rainy Saturday morning. He peered through the small diamond-shaped window and saw Toby standing on his doorstep, nervously eyeing the wild geese that lived there in the pond. The geese were honking, upright, and flapping their wings territorially. He could see that Toby was anxious to step inside. Mickey smirked at his distress but opened the door.

"When are you going to get rid of those geese, Mickey? They're a menace."

"You know I've tried. Don't you remember the police chief paying me a visit to tell me I couldn't shoot at them 'cause they were within five hundred feet of a residence? Even if it was my own damn house?"

"Yeah."

"Well, now my only hope is that the coyotes will get them."

Toby scraped his wet shoes on the doormat and took off his wet raincoat, draping it over his arm. "Any word from our friend Denton?"

"Yeah. The little coward."

Toby looked over at him fixedly. "What'd he say?"

"Says he can't do it." Mickey pulled a sour face as he made his way back to his blue leather couch. He plopped down on one end, reached to the glass coffee table for a handful of nuts, then stuffed his mouth with all of them.

Toby sat in a leather end chair and waited until Mickey was ready to explain. He still held his raincoat, dripping, in one hand.

"Clarisse!" yelled Mickey.

"What?" came a faint voice from a distant part of the house.

"C'mere, would'ja?"

Mickey and Toby heard footsteps on the stairs coming up from the basement. Clarisse swung the cellar door open into the kitchen and began walking towards the living room. "Oh, hi, Toby. What's up, Mickey?"

"As you can see, we have a guest. Can you hang up Toby's raincoat and then get us a coupla coffees?"

Clarisse scowled at them. "Toby's not a guest: he's here every other day. And you know the coffee's already brewed and waiting in the pot."

"But you're so much cuter than me, mixing it up. And Toby's coat is dripping wet." Mickey gave her a wink.

Clarisse rolled her eyes, but held out a hand to take Toby's raincoat. "I was in the basement getting up a load of laundry when you called me." She padded off to the kitchen with the raincoat and soon returned with a tray of cups, a carafe of coffee, a pitcher of cream, the sugar bowl, spoons, and biscuits.

"That's my girl," said Mickey as he smiled up at her.

"Don't worry, I'll charge it to your credit card next time I'm at the mall," she said.

"Fresh broad, you are!"

"You said you liked 'em young and fresh! That's

me!" Clarisse turned on her heel, walked to the kitchen, opened the cellar door, and went back downstairs.

Mickey looked at Toby who was eyeing him steadily. "The thing about Clarisse," said Mickey, "is that she talks big, but she always does what I want her to do."

"If you say so."

"What do you know? You've only been married for some twenty years!"

"That just makes me realize, more than ever, that women are unpredictable."

Mickey took a bite from a biscuit then a slurp from his coffee. He pursed his lips as he looked down. "Enough about broads."

"Okay. Then tell me what the *little coward* said." Toby began to chew on the fingernail of his index finger rather than a biscuit. No wonder he was so skinny, Mickey thought.

"Denton said he couldn't find a reason for Longbottom Savings Bank to foreclose on the Jaston loan. He said they were all paid up. All up to date."

Toby drew his lips together into a thin line. "I was hoping it wouldn't come to this."

"Come to what?"

"A political solution," said Toby.

"What do you mean?"

"There's another way to get ahold of the Jaston land, and it's legal, but it'll involve the local politicians."

"Who?"

"The selectmen," said Toby.

"Why them?"

"Because they're the lawfully elected executive branch under the Open Town Meeting form of government."

"What will they have to do?"

"They'll have to seize the land under eminent domain." Toby stared at Mickey to see if he understood him. Mickey was staring down into his half-filled cup, as if the answer could be found in the swirls of creamy coffee.

"Can they do that?" he asked, craning his neck to look at Toby.

"They can."

"But how? We're only a bunch of businessmen. Not the government. I thought only the government could take land by eminent domain."

Toby grinned at him widely, exposing his row of long, yellowed teeth. "Ah, my friend! You know you would have made a fine lawyer if you hadn't decided to do your own thing. You know your talents are wasted at that pub."

"That's old news. Meanwhile, how can we, private businessmen, get the Jaston land by eminent domain?"

"You have the U.S. Supreme Court to thank for that," said Toby.

"By a case they decided?"

"Exactly."

"Wow."

"You said it, bud."

"Sounds pretty radical, actually," said Mickey. He was silent for a long moment. "I wouldn't want anyone to try to use it against my house or my business."

"It would never happen."

"Why?"

"Look at who you are. The selectmen would never vote to take your land."

Mickey was silent again, thinking. "Do you think we can persuade them to take the Jaston land?"

"Sure. Just cut them in on the deal." Toby grinned again.

"I guess you're right. Money talks," said Mickey.

"Money walks," said Toby. "Money will get the Jastons to leave their land."

CHAPTER 6

"The sons of bitches have arrived!" announced Mickey Quinn to the room at large. He craned his neck to peer out of the window of his living room from his seat on the blue leather couch.

"Mickey!" said Clarisse. "Is that any way to talk about our elected officials?"

"Why not? If they've been elected, it means they're bigger bastards than most."

"Well somebody liked them. They got elected, didn't they?"

"Yeah, by their relatives and friends. And since everybody is related to everybody in this town, that's no achievement."

"Well you're a townie, Mickey," Clarisse pointed out.

"Yeah, but I marry out-of-towners, like you. Too much inbreeding going on if you ask me. Gotta introduce some new blood."

"Mickey, I see you're not in your best mood right now," said Toby, "but may I urge you to adopt your usual charm-offensive. We need the selectmen's cooperation, odious as it may be."

Mickey pursed his lips together and stared hard out the window. "I see Gerald Hopper's driving a new Jeep. Lipstick red for the lover boy."

"I thought the lover-boy was Danny Tripiano," said Toby. "Wasn't he the one that got caught by the

31

woman's husband in the bedroom and had to run out of the house bare-ass naked?"

Mickey cackled at the image Toby's words conjured up. "You're right. Scrappy little Danny-boy was always tooling around town with his appliance repair truck to all the housewives of Longbottom."

"You two are worse gossipers than any woman I know," said Clarisse.

"Never mind us, sweetie," said Mickey. "Just be sure you mix those margaritas good and strong for the selectmen."

Clarisse went back to the kitchen while Mickey and Toby watched the three selectmen get out of the Jeep tentatively. None of the newly elected selectmen had been to Mickey Quinn's house before, and they stood in the driveway, eyeing the property for a long moment. The Quinn house was huge, built on a rise, with elaborate landscaping on wide grounds. Across the street from his house were deep woods.

The flock of wild geese that had taken up residence on his side of the street began stirring from their position near his pond. At one time he had stocked the pond with koi and had planted lily pads. The koi pond had been his vanity. But then the geese had invaded, bringing their excrement with them, slowly poisoning the koi, causing them to turn belly-up one by one. Toby had commented, "Life is shit, and then you die, in the lonely life of a koi." Mickey had not been amused. In fact, it was shortly thereafter that he had taken up shooting at the geese.

Now they watched Gerald Hopper, Danny Tripiano,

and Marilyn Hardy eye the geese apprehensively as they walked up the brick walkway to the front entrance. Distantly, the geese were honking and beginning to move towards them. Gerald Hopper rang the doorbell, waited a moment, and rang it a second time, a bit urgently, it seemed.

Clarisse took pity on them and opened the door. The three selectmen trooped in and stood just inside the foyer. They looked into the spacious living room furnished with blue leather seating and a huge blue and white oriental rug over a hardwood floor.

"I'm over here," said Mickey, from the depths of the couch. "Welcome to my humble abode." He stood up, and approached them with his right hand outstretched to shake their hands, one by one. "My trusted legal advisor, Tobias Meachum, is here, too. I hope that's okay with you folks."

"Of course," said Gerald Hopper immediately, and the other two grunted their assent.

"Can I get you three anything to eat or drink? I've got some sandwiches and a pitcher of margaritas," said Clarisse.

"A margarita sounds great," said Danny Tripiano.

Marilyn Hardy gave him a withering look. "I'll start with a sandwich, Clarisse, if you don't mind; it's only noon."

"I have tuna and I have ham and cheese."

"I'll have the ham and cheese, please."

"I'll bring the tray out, and you can help yourselves," said Clarisse. "I'm bringing out the pitcher of margaritas and the glasses, too. Take a seat,

33

everyone."

The three selectmen arranged themselves in the leather seats and couch and got comfortable. They began surveying the room.

Marilyn Hardy noticed the bookcases, devoid of books but full of photos of Mickey and his current wife with friends and family and a few art objects scattered in between. *How often did Mickey Quinn have to change his array of photos?* thought Marilyn Hardy. They probably changed with each new wife. New wife, new life. She wondered if he stashed away photos of his ex-wives or discarded or destroyed them. That would be an interesting question to ask him, she thought. A testament to his character, whichever way he answered.

Gerald Hopper noticed the big, flat-screen TV. *Mickey Quinn has got those big flat screen TV's in his bar that he can watch all day if he wants, but I wonder if he watches TV or his wife when he gets home*, Gerald Hopper thought. *She's a juicy piece. And can make a tasty margarita, to boot,* he thought, sipping his drink gratefully. He decided that Mickey Quinn didn't properly appreciate his lovely wife and, given the opportunity, he would do much, much better. He looked down at the carpet to conceal his thoughts.

Danny Tripiano was two-fisted, with his margarita in one hand and a tuna fish sandwich in the other. He was oblivious to his surroundings, instead concentrating on the food and drink before him. The more he sipped on the margarita, the more his wide face with its big prow of a Roman nose began to look lightly flushed. His dark eyes, deep in his head, got smaller the more he drank.

He looks like a clown, thought Mickey Quinn, noting Danny Tripiano's big head atop the skinny body, and the black hair extruding from his ears. *God knows what the women of Longbottom see in him.*

And Gerald Hopper is no better, thought Mickey. *He wears those fancy polo shirts and gets those fancy haircuts like he's some kind of movie star. And he's always trying to steal my best waitresses for his lousy pizza joint.*

"You're probably wondering why I called you all over to my house," said Mickey.

"Kinda," said Danny, pushing the remnants of a sandwich into his mouth.

"I figured on a friendly game of Russian roulette. Whoever's left standing gets my house and my bar. I'll go get my pistol."

There was dead silence.

"Well, that broke the ice," Mickey Quinn said with a deadpan voice.

Still, no one moved or said a word.

"Geeze, you people have no sense of humor," said Mickey.

"What's going on, Mickey?" asked Gerald Hopper.

"I got a way for you people to all get rich, and you don't have to kill me to do it."

"That's more like it, Mickey," said Danny Tripiano, heaving a big breath.

"Had you going there, huh, Danny?"

"Kinda," Danny admitted.

"Alright. Can any of you geniuses think of any

parcels of open land left in Longbottom?" asked Mickey.

"The state forest," Danny answered.

Mickey Quinn rolled his eyes. "That can't be developed, genius."

"The Jaston farm," said Marilyn Hardy.

"Bonus points for the lady," said Mickey, looking at the tawny-haired, angular woman who had helped herself to her first margarita, despite her initial disapproval.

"What's my prize?" she asked.

"Your share of the profits."

"Of what?"

"The development that'll be on the Jaston farm."

"Hey," said Danny. "What about us?"

"Are you being greedy, Mr. Tripiano?"

"Darn right I am."

"Well, it's your lucky day, Danny. You get to be included. All of you selectmen."

"Just what are we included in?" asked Gerald Hopper, suddenly feeling sober.

"A company wants to come in and build a big money casino in this part of the state. The company needs land."

"What company?"

"Never mind what company right now. One of the big boys."

"Where do we come in?"

"Toby will explain that part," said Mickey.

Tobias Meachum sat forward in his chair and slowly looked at each of them. "Have any of you heard of a recent case called *Kelo vs. the City of New London, Connecticut?*"

Everyone looked at one another, wonderingly.

Toby continued. "The U.S. Supreme Court has ruled in the past that governments can take property from people by eminent domain for public purposes. We all know that." He raised his right hand for emphasis. "What's new is this: now, 'taken' property can be turned over to another private individual or private corporation. The only requirement is that the private party has to bring something called 'substantial economic development' to the community."

"So you're saying that land can be taken from X and given to Y, 'cause Y is going to bring more jobs and pay more taxes...is that right?" asked Gerald Hopper.

"You got it," said Tobias Meachum.

"That's horrible!" said Gerald Hopper. "That's not fair!

"What's not fair about it?" asked Toby, scratching his pointed chin.

"It was X's land to begin with," said Gerald Hopper.

"X will get paid for his land. It's not like they're taking it away without any compensation at all," Toby replied smoothly.

"But maybe X didn't want to sell. Maybe he wanted to keep doing what he was doing," argued Gerald Hopper.

"What does this all have to do with the Jaston farm?" asked Danny.

Gerald Hopper turned to him in exasperation.

"That's the piece of land they're thinking of 'taking' for this casino."

"Oh," said Danny, the situation beginning to reveal itself to him.

"It's the only parcel of land left that's large enough for a casino," explained Toby.

"But why eminent domain?" asked Gerald Hopper. "Why not just buy it off them?"

"Easier said than done, my friend," said Toby. "They refuse to sell."

"Did you offer them enough money?"

"Millions," said Mickey. "They were stuck on the concept of selling."

"You probably didn't approach them the right way," chided Danny.

"I doubt you would have been more successful, Danny. Anyway, if we had gotten them to sell, we wouldn't be here discussing the matter with you three. And you three wouldn't have had the chance to cash in on the deal. So what do you care?"

"I still think eminent domain seems kinda drastic," said Gerald Hopper. "I'm kinda taking it personally, being a property owner of a business and all."

"How does the eminent domain actually happen?" asked Danny.

"Ah, a practical question at last," said Toby. "The actual process is simple. You three take a vote to 'take' the land, and it's done. You three are, after all, the executive branch of the local government."

"That's it? Just a vote?" asked Danny.

"That's it," said Tobias Meachum. "At one of your

38

selectmen's meetings, of course."

"It'll be on cable TV. They'll see us take the vote," said Danny.

"Of course they will. Some poor suckers in town without a life always watch the meetings," said Toby.

"I don't think it'll fly politically," said Marilyn Hardy, speaking up for the first time, sipping on her second margarita.

"Why not?" asked Danny.

"Because the Jaston farm has been in this town for a hundred years or more," said Gerald Hopper. "The Jastons are well-known and liked. Old Man Jaston was a selectman in his day, if I remember right." He fingered his moustache nervously.

Mickey watched him playing with his moustache and recalled that Gerald had once drunkenly referred to it as his "tickler" and claimed it was the secret to his success with the ladies. Mickey rolled his eyes at the memory.

"If we're gonna be taking this risk politically, what's in it for us?" Danny asked pointedly.

Well we finally reached the nub of it, thought Mickey. He nodded to Toby to proceed.

"Gentlemen, and lady," said Toby, "we're prepared to cut each of you in on a one percent share of the net profits."

"For?" asked Danny.

"Voting to 'take' the land by eminent domain. I thought that was already clear."

"Big deal! One percent!" said Danny.

"That's fair," said Marilyn Hardy, who was pouring

herself a third margarita. "As I see it, the land is underutilized by a bunch of cows."

"Those cows do produce milk. For people like schoolchildren," said Gerald. "And chocolate factories."

"Spare me the Willy Wonka sentiments, please! Those cows are tying up an enormous tract of land," said Marilyn Hardy. "And the only ones employed on it are the Jastons and a few seasonal workers."

"Never mind all that," said Danny. "What I want to know is how much money does this one percent amount to?"

"Hundreds of thousands a year," said Toby, breaking out into a wide smile that showed his long, yellow teeth.

Mickey watched their reactions. Gerald Hopper's head tilted to one side inquisitively and he abruptly closed his mouth. He began vigorously stroking his moustache again while staring at the carpet. Marilyn Hardy drew in her breath sharply and held her margarita aloft, not moving. Danny Tripiano began to smile, broadly, while repeating, "Hot damn!"

Mickey sat on the edge of the couch, watching Gerald wrestle with his conscience. He waited, fairly confident which side would win out. And he had the other two ready to act on his behalf anyway.

"You in, Jerry?" asked Mickey Quinn, softly.

Gerald closed his eyes and the corners of his mouth turned down. In a strangled voice he said, "I'm in."

CHAPTER 7

The unblinking eye of the camera focused on the inspirational portraits of George Washington and Abraham Lincoln affixed high up on the wood-paneled wall while the piped-in classical music from the radio played over the airwaves to the viewers at home.

The meeting was due to start, but the selectmen weren't ready. The cameraman accommodated them by keeping them off-camera.

The high-ceiling room of Town Hall could, at best, fit twenty citizens inside, since the room was mainly occupied by the huge solid oak table and high-backed leather chairs reserved for the selectmen. The rest of the citizens of Longbottom were encouraged to stay home, where they could watch the meetings from a conveniently distant outpost, such as their living room couch, where expressions of dissent would not be heard.

The three selectmen adjusted their expressions to those of attention and concern as they took their seats facing the few townspeople. The cable television camera swung downward to capture their images, and the meeting opened.

"Beginning this meeting," said Marilyn Hardy in a dainty voice, "is the matter of Mrs. Amelia Little's sign for her dog-grooming business. Gerald? Do you want to handle this?"

Gerald Hopper started by clearing his throat. "Okay. Mrs. Little? How large a sign do you propose to erect in front of your business?"

"I want a twenty foot by thirty foot sign," said Mrs. Little, visibly nervous, "and I want it in neon, with the image of a dog paw out-lining the sign."

"Well, it takes all kinds," chuckled Gerald Hopper.

"I hope not," interrupted a lanky young woman with straw-yellow hair who stood in the back of the room. "My house is next door to her business, and my bedroom faces the street where her sign will be. It'll be like a red-light district with that thing out there!"

"Young lady, you're out of order," said Marilyn Hardy. "You haven't been asked to speak."

"I'm an abutter," said the young woman. "I have a right to object to that sign!"

"It's my business venture," said Mrs. Little. "I need to make my business visible to the community!"

"That sign is gonna be garish and ugly!" exclaimed the young woman. "Isn't there some kind of town bylaw limiting what size a sign can be?"

Marilyn Hardy began banging her gavel against the oak table. "Young lady, if you persist in speaking out of turn, you'll have to be removed from the meeting. Is that clear?"

"For your information, young lady, Longbottom has yet to pass a town bylaw regulating the size and type of sign a business may erect in front of its building. Therefore Mrs. Little's request to the Board of Selectmen is perfectly in order," said Gerald Hopper. He swiveled his head to look at the other two. "All in favor?" he said.

"Aye!" said all three selectmen.

"You're letting her put up a ridiculous sign 'cause she's lived in town her whole life, and I'm a newcomer," said the young woman loudly. The camera swung around to capture her angry image.

"Don't make accusations like that, that have no basis in fact," Gerald responded, his normally lightly tanned face suffused pink with anger.

The young woman tossed her straw-yellow hair defiantly and marched out of the room.

"Thank you," said Mrs. Little. "Thank you." She nearly bowed in gratitude.

"Don't mention it, Mrs. Little," said Gerald Hopper who was visibly calming down. "What's next on the agenda?" He adjusted his shirt collar and looked at Marilyn Hardy.

"We have to appoint an interim tree warden," she replied. "We have two candidates seeking the position. Danny, why don't you handle this one?"

"Will the two candidates please step forward?" said Danny Tripiano.

Two men who were sitting quietly in the crowd rose and came forward. "You, sir," pointed Danny Tripiano to the one in front of him. "State your name and qualifications, please."

"I'm Joe Davies," said a thin, muscular man of middle height with a salt-and-pepper mustache. "I work at a local nursery where they sell trees, as well as other plants, and I work part-time in an orchard."

"And you, sir?" asked Danny Tripiano.

"I'm Ray Wolford," said a bespectacled, short, heavy man. "I'm from the Wolford family of

Longbottom, and I'm an experienced gardener. I think you know my family, Mr. Tripiano."

"Yes, I believe I do. Gardening, you say. That's very good. Any discussion?"

"We need to consider all factors, including a person's roots - pardon the pun - when making our decision," said Marilyn Hardy. "A person who lives in town can be an asset in an emergency."

"I live in the next town over, so I'm easily called in on an emergency," said Joe Davies. "Plus I think work in an orchard and at a nursery are better qualifications."

Marilyn Hardy looked over at him and smiled blandly. She turned back to Danny Tripiano. "I move we appoint Ray Wolford."

"Second," said Danny Tripiano. "All in favor?"

"Aye," all three said simultaneously.

"Congratulations, Ray, you're the new tree warden," said Danny Tripiano. "Give my regards to your mother."

"Thank you, I will. Thanks for your vote of support, everyone!" He pushed his eyeglasses up his broad nose then made his move to leave.

Joe Davies abruptly turned on his heel and headed for the door. Once in the hallway, he leaned against a doorjamb and eyed the others sardonically while tapping an unlit cigarette against the wall. "That's a kangaroo court in there," he muttered to no one in particular.

"Now we have some administrative matters to attend to," said Marilyn Hardy. "Just some routine paperwork." She picked up a sheaf of papers that were laying to her left and began leafing through them.

"A business opportunity has come to Longbottom, and therefore the town needs to assign some land over to that purpose."

"What land?" called out one of the seated townspeople.

Marilyn Hardy ignored the question and began to read from the sheaf of papers.

"I am proposing that land consisting of Lots 497, 498, 499, 500, 501, and 502, within the jurisdiction of Longbottom, be taken by eminent domain on behalf of a business called Investment Opportunities, for the purpose of promoting business development in Longbottom."

"What land?" repeated the citizen, who was now standing in front of his folding chair. "Why aren't we being told what land it is?"

The camera swung around to reveal a tall, craggy man wearing a rust-colored corduroy jacket and blue jeans.

"You're out of order, Mr. Rutherford," said Marilyn Hardy. "I'm not finished yet." She looked back down at her papers and resumed reading. "Whereas now the land is under tax exemption, the betterments to such land shall be assessed at the business rate of taxation, which will increase revenue to the town. As there are trees and structures upon said land, they shall be included in the taking, but the owner shall have the reasonable time of six months to relocate his personal effects." Marilyn Hardy looked up from her papers and turned to the other two selectmen. "The owners of said land will be compensated in an amount equal to fair market value, to

45

be determined by an appraisal." Once more, she looked up from her papers and looked at the other two selectmen. "I propose that the taking by eminent domain be done by vote of this board of selectmen tonight."

"I think you three selectmen are out of order," said Mr. Rutherford. "Just whose land are you taking by eminent domain?"

"Not yours, Mr. Rutherford, don't worry," said Danny Tripiano with a grin. The camera caught him tugging on a hairy ear as he sat chuckling.

"All in favor?" said Marilyn Hardy.

"Aye!" said all three together, a little too forcefully.

A whispering sound rose in the room from all the onlookers as they speculated on who the unlucky landowner might be. The camera remained strictly on the three selectmen.

"Seeing no other business before us, I move to adjourn," said Danny Tripiano.

The camera instantly flicked back to the portraits of George Washington and Abraham Lincoln while the piped-in music began.

The meeting was over. What the people at home could not see, but perhaps sensed, were that knots of people lingered after the meeting, stunned by what they had just witnessed. The unsettling ramifications of that vote were felt by all of those who had been in the selectmen's meeting as they pondered their place in town government and upon freedoms won and lost. However, they were disorganized, despairing, disheartened. No one began to protest. Some looked at one another shamefacedly while others kept their eyes on the floor. Someone would have to do something. But what? And who?

The townspeople continued to murmur dejectedly amongst themselves for some time until, at last, the night janitor chased them out of the building.

CHAPTER 8

Robert Jaston hadn't heard anything in a while from Mickey Quinn or Tobias Meachum. He began to have a sliver of hope that they weren't going to go after their farm after all. Still, he worried that the scent of money was in their nostrils like a fresh kill. He knew wolves never loosen their grip on their prey once they got it between their teeth.

Robert came in from the barn at mid-day for lunch, and took off his boots before coming into the kitchen. He knew something was wrong when he looked at Maureen. Her normally pink face had turned chalky white. She was staring down at a single piece of paper clutched in her hand. She hadn't made a sound. It was as if time stopped, or maybe he felt her heart dropping in her chest, in sympathy. He lurched forward to steady her.

"Robert," she muttered hoarsely, dropping the paper in front of him onto the kitchen table. "Read this."

It was short and brutal. The paper was called "Order of Taking". It said that Longbottom claimed their land by eminent domain, that they were to be compensated for the land and effects in the amount of 1.2 million dollars, and they had six months to get off the premises.

Who are they kidding? thought Robert. *What about my cows, my milking equipment, my barn, my tractor? Not to mention the house. What about the land? They're nothing more'n a bunch of thieves as far as I'm concerned.*

Reading those words was like putting an ice pick into Robert's head; the worst headache he could remember began just then.

Robert looked back at Maureen. Color had come back to her face and neck. Now she was flushed and her gray-blue eyes blazed. "How dare they do this to us?" she said.

Just then, the twin girls, Layla and Shaina came running up to the kitchen door, panting. "Mommy, Mommy, you've got to come see the new litter of kittens just born in the barn. Come right now!" They pressed their faces flat against the screen door to see into the kitchen while fidgeting on the granite doorstep.

"Girls, your father and I have something important to talk about now," Maureen said irritably.

Robert could see, even with his headache moving to form behind his right eye, that the girls were downcast. "Sweetheart," he said, not wanting to get on her bad side for fear that tonight all he'd get was her backside, "Maureen, honey, we won't solve this problem in the next ten minutes. Let's go to the barn with the girls."

Maureen relented with his gentle tone. *Handling Maureen is like dealing with a frisky pony,* thought Robert. *Needs a steady hand and a steady heart. But still there's nobody like her, nobody more sexy than this woman who still walks with head held up high and the gait of a young girl. Motherhood hasn't broken her. Nor has being a wife. She still has some of the girl in her.*

As they all traipsed down to the barn, Robert began

remembering how he and Maureen had met in front of the punchbowl table at the Longbottom Homecoming Dance.

Robert smiled to himself as he remembered that they had both gone with different dates. He with a quiet girl named Lily, who was pretty enough but didn't really do it for him. It had been rumored that Lily liked him, so he had invited her to the dance. Lily wore a light blue shiny dress that fit her narrow body tightly. She was blonde and fair and dipped her head whenever he tried to joke with her. She didn't have much to say for herself, but she paid close attention to him, so he guessed she did like him.

Maureen had a track runner named Jonathan as her date. He had been skinny as a string bean with a mop of curly brown hair. He had squired her around a bit, then he went to stand in the corner with his co-athletes to talk about track meets.

Robert remembered he first saw Maureen from behind, noticing her beautiful red-brown hair curling down her back to her waist. Maureen later told him the color was called auburn. He had noticed her waist and hips and legs. He wanted to see if the face and front were as good as the back. She turned just then, and he saw her.

The moment he saw her pretty face, he knew she was the one.

Robert walked over to introduce himself. He knew his words had to be just right.

He could tell she was a sassy thing, and he needed to say something bold. So he said, "Was that you skinny-dipping in our pond last summer?"

Maureen had laughed hard, turning pink, and said, "You've got a pond?"

"Yes."

"How do you happen to have a pond? You must have an awfully big yard."

"My family owns a farm, actually."

"Oh." She had tilted her head as she considered this. "Do you go skinny-dipping?"

"Only with the right people. Or with the right person." He had looked deep into her eyes, and she had blushed, then laughed.

"What kind of farmer are you, anyway?" she asked.

"A dairy farmer. I'm Robert Jaston."

"I'm Maureen Carson."

"How come I've never met you before? I thought I knew everyone in town," said Robert.

"I'm new to town. We moved here two weeks ago. My father is the new pharmacist at the Longbottom drug store.

"You'll have to come see my farm. It's mighty pretty. Just like you."

"I bet you talk to all the girls this way."

"Actually, never." He had looked directly in her eyes again. "And every word is true. Would you like to dance?"

"What about our dates?"

"What about them?"

"What'll they think if we start dancing with each other?"

"They'll realize they're outta luck."

51

She had laughed again, throwing her head back, showing her long, slim neck. "Let's do it!"

Just as they had hit the dance floor, as if specially ordered, the lights had gone low and the mirrored ball on the ceiling sent white stars orbiting around the walls. They were slow-dancing in each other's arms, discovering they were the perfect size and height for each other. Robert remembered that Maureen felt right in his arms. Her hair had floated in the air around them, brushing his hands like the gossamer wings of dragonflies. He knew that Maureen was elemental to him, like soil, sun, and water. The farmer in him knew.

Robert smiled again, remembering. As it had turned out, both Lily and Jonathan had been peeved at them since they had gone on to monopolize each other for the rest of the night. Lily was still mad at him, even after all these years.

They had been married in the Congregational church in Longbottom on a hot summer's day. The wedding reception had been held in the hay barn, on the farm. A fiddler led the country band which played square dance tunes. The guests had clinked on their wine glasses with their forks repeatedly, making them kiss each other over and over.

After the meal the elderly exchanged stories at the long wooden tables while the children scattered to chase one another outside the barn. The party had gone on until two a.m.

During their honeymoon phase, they had gone down to the pond night after night to go skinny-dipping. Maureen had made him promise to take her there for that purpose. One thing led to another, as they say.

Maureen was forever convinced that their son Jacob was conceived that first night. In later years, when she looked at their son's inner glow, she said she believed it came from his being conceived by moonlight and called him her moonchild.

Our twin girls are another matter, thought Robert. *If Jacob is a moonchild, they are children of sunlight: bright, direct, without guile. They are a joy to behold, with their jokes, riddles, and gossip. They have made our home a place of openness and honesty.*

"Look, Daddy. Snowball's got six kittens! When we came to the house to get you, she only had five! She had another one while we were up at the house!" said Shaina.

"Mommy, Daddy, can we keep the kittens? We don't have to give them away, do we?" asked Layla.

"We'll have to give away some of them, girls. But you can pick your favorites to keep," said Maureen. "We want the good mousers, though. You know the saying: 'Everybody on the farm works'. Right?"

"Yes, Mommy," they chorused.

"You've been awfully quiet," said Maureen, looking at Robert.

"I've just been remembering some of our early times together, and the early days on the farm as a young couple," Robert said.

"Those were very good days," she said wistfully. "And they may come to an untimely end if this eminent domain nonsense goes through."

"I know. I've got a horrible headache from it. But

I've gotta tackle this problem straight on. Any suggestions?"

"Let's go back up to the house and discuss it," said Maureen. "Little ears and all that, you know."

"You're right. Come on." They started up the path to the farmhouse.

All too soon, they were back at the kitchen table, staring at that hated notice.

"So, are you going to let this farm be taken away from you?" asked Maureen.

"No way," Robert responded. "I'll go down fighting if I have to."

"Good," said Maureen. "Now do you want to call a lawyer, or should I?"

"Let me take some aspirin, and then I'll make some calls," he told her.

CHAPTER 9

"How about some grilled cheese sandwiches for everyone?" said Maureen.

"Always choose a dairy product when you can!" intoned Robert in a sing-song voice.

"Well-spoken, dairy-man," answered Maureen, pertly rhyming.

"Good one, honey," he said. That got Maureen to smile, at least.

After lunch, Robert got busy with the telephone book. He spent a good bit of time studying the ads, trying to figure out whether each lawyer was a straight-shooter or a money-grubber. It was impossible to tell, based on the ads alone, he realized. He would have to speak to each one in person.

Robert called the first one, a Mr. Harris, who had his office in the neighboring town. Mr. Harris came on the phone, and listened as Robert told him about his farm and the eminent domain. He sounded interested. Then Robert told him that Mickey Quinn and Tobias Meachum were behind it all, and Mr. Harris cooled off quickly. Mr. Harris told Robert it would take 50 grand to litigate the case.

"I don't have that kind of cash lying around, Mr. Harris."

"You can always take out a mortgage on your property to pay my fee," suggested Mr. Harris.

"I'll think about it, and get back to you," said

Robert, while putting a big X through his ad.

He tried four other lawyers, but every one of them got squirrelly when they heard about Mickey Quinn and Tobias Meachum being involved. It was as if they knew the fix was in up at the courthouse, and they had no chance from the start. Two of them asked Robert for big fees, regardless.

Maureen was at Robert's side, listening to his end of the conversation. She could tell he was getting discouraged. Finally, she said, "Let it rest, Robert. We won't settle this today. In the meantime, it's time for the afternoon milking."

Robert left the table and phone behind and set out for the barn. Out in the barn, the heat rising off the cows' bodies attracted circling summer flies. Cow tails flicked to and fro listlessly. The cows' teats were swollen from pent-up milk, and they seemed to enjoy the relief the milking machine provided them. He went through his twice-daily routine yet again, wiping down each teat with disinfectant before attaching the suction hose. Then he fell into his usual daze, waiting, as the pure white milk was slowly piped over to the holding tank.

Robert didn't know what he was supposed to do with his cows, with this eminent domain looming over him. Sell them, he guessed. But to whom? There were only about 180 dairy farms left in Massachusetts these days, down from 7000 or so, when he had started farming with his father. There just weren't many farmers to sell to anymore. And he had no idea where he'd get the land to start up another dairy farm. If it was even worth it. What with milk prices so low. But he couldn't face Maureen if he just gave up now. She would look at him as if he had given up his manhood. And that would happen when hell froze over, he told himself.

Robert returned to the house from the barn more agitated than when he left. His shirt collar chafed on his neck in the summer swelter. The barn had been hotter than a furnace, it seemed, with motes of hay floating in the air, tickling his throat, making him cough. He needed a glass of Maureen's cold, sweet lemonade to soothe his mouth and throat. He felt so hot and dirty just now, he was ready to jump out of his own skin. He took off his boots inside the doorstep, and walked further into the kitchen in his stocking feet. "Hi, honey," he said. "Have you made any calls to any lawyers?"

"A couple," said Maureen. "No luck with the establishment lawyers. They're all too scared for their reputations to take on Mickey Quinn and Tobias Meachum."

Robert pursed his lips and lowered his eyes. He sat down heavily at the kitchen table. "Where does that leave us?"

"With a young, inexperienced, female lawyer named Anna Ebert as the only one who will take this case."

Robert sniffed. He wiped his nose with the back of his hand. "Hand me a glass of lemonade, would you, honey?"

"So whaddya think? Should we go with this young lady lawyer? asked Maureen.

"Maybe," said Robert, after a long slow drink of

lemonade. "I'd like to meet her, first, before we just sign on with her."

"Of course, Robert. We won't take her if she's some kind of flake or a nut-job."

"Did you make an appointment with her?"

"Yep. For tomorrow, at ten a.m. You'll be long done with morning milking and have had time to wash up, and Jacob can watch the girls while we're gone."

"Where's her office?"

"Off the town common, on the second floor, over the pet store."

"Okay, babe. Looks like you've got matters well in hand. What's for dinner?"

"Just an omelet, sweetie. I was a little too upset to get together a regular dinner."

"You and me both."

"Girls! Jacob! Dinner's ready! Come wash your hands!" bellowed Maureen suddenly.

Robert flinched. "I thought you'd tear my ears off with that yelling," he said.

"Only way to get 'em to the table. You know that."

"Yep. I married a real, honest-to-goodness lady, I did."

"And for that you can count your blessings," said Maureen.

CHAPTER 10

"Are we gonna have to get dressed up for this meeting with the lawyer?" asked Robert. "Cause I'd rather just go in my overalls."

"Honey, just put on a clean pair of jeans and a clean shirt, and you'll be fine. This isn't a job interview. We're hiring her. Maybe. We'll see." Maureen applied a bit of mascara and lip gloss, and ran her fingers through her long auburn hair. They were both trying to see in the dresser mirror in their upstairs bedroom, and mostly getting in each other's way. Maureen glanced out the window and saw that this day was going to be another scorcher, even though it was only June, and the kids had just gotten out of school for the summer break.

Robert looked at his watch. "Come on, honey. Any more primping, and we'll be late."

Layla and Shaina were lurking in the hallway outside their bedroom, peeking around the doorway. They were wondering what all the fuss was about on a weekday.

"We've got some business in town, girls. If you need anything, you ask Jacob. Stay in the house while we're gone. That means don't go in the barn. Not even to see Snowball. I mean it. Okay?" said Maureen.

Okay, Mommy," they said together.

"Jacob!" yelled Maureen.

"What, Ma?" came his voice from downstairs.

"Look alive! Your sisters need tending to. I'm

holding you responsible!"

"Okay, Ma." His voice floated upstairs.

Maureen grabbed her purse, and began hurrying down the stairs. She reached for the Notice of the "Order of Taking", folded it, and carefully placed it in her purse. "That means getting up off the couch, away from your video game, and over to where your sisters are, to see what they're up to." She punched the remote to shut off the television.

Jacob was fourteen, black haired and black eyed like his father, and was big and raw-boned for his age. He had a hint of a moustache on his upper lip that he cultivated, along with a deliberately heavy-lidded, sidelong look that he gave to his little sisters when they were particularly annoying. He sighed heavily, but got up off the couch, and went upstairs.

Robert was waiting in the kitchen, truck keys looped around his index finger.

"Everything okay?"

"Just dandy."

They got in their seven-year-old red Ford truck and fastened their seatbelts. Robert turned the radio on the country music station automatically, without thinking. Maureen hated country music, but said nothing. They pulled out of their curved gravel driveway and set off for the town center.

They parked on the street in front of Anna Ebert's office. They saw a small hanging sign with her name on it and an arrow pointing to the second floor. They went into the stairwell and began climbing the stairs. The stairs were shabbily carpeted, visibly dusty, and very steep. At the top was a small landing which led to a door with a glass window. Inside, they could see a middle-aged buxom blonde woman at a computer.

When the woman saw them, she gestured for them to come inside.

"Hello. I'm Trudy. I'm the office manager for Attorney Anna Ebert. I'll let her know you're here." She rose from her swivel chair and went into the office behind her.

Trudy returned in a moment and said, "Go right in."

Robert and Maureen walked into a surprisingly spacious office that had tall windows in the back that looked out over the rear of the building, and into the branches of an airy linden tree.

"What a nice view," said Maureen. "Who would've thought from the front of the building?"

"Appearances can be deceiving," replied Anna Ebert, a wide smile on her thin face. She stood up behind her enormous desk, a tiny woman in a tailored suit. She walked out to greet them, her right hand outstretched to grasp theirs in a handshake.

She had shoulder-length black hair, green eyes, and pale, clear skin. "I'm Attorney Ebert. How can I help you?" She looked no more than twenty years old.

"We're Robert and Maureen Jaston," said Robert. "My wife spoke to you yesterday."

"Yes. Come in, and tell me your problem."

Robert and Maureen followed her into her office, where they found two uncomfortable wooden chairs placed in front of the enormous desk. They sat. Maureen planted her hefty purse on her lap, and drew out the wrinkled notice. Without a word, she handed it to Anna Ebert to read.

"When did you get this notice?" asked Anna Ebert.

"Yesterday," said Robert. "Maureen opened the mail."

"It gives you six months to be out. And it offers you 1.2 million, if you take it."

"Bastards." said Robert, not caring to hide his feelings. "We're not about to take the money and run."

"From what I've read up on, the law of eminent domain is stacked against you," said Anna Ebert. "The recent case of *Kelo vs. The City of New London* put an undue amount of power in the hands of local municipal authorities." Her mouth turned grim.

Robert jutted his lower jaw as he waited to hear more.

"I heard through the town grapevine that the selectmen had voted to take somebody's land by eminent domain, but nobody knew who was the unlucky one." Anna Ebert tapped her pen on her pad of paper. "Sorry it was you. Sorry it was anybody. They had no business doing that to anybody in town."

"So what can we do?" asked Maureen.

"We have to fight fire with fire," said Anna Ebert.

"What do you mean?" said Maureen.

"What I mean," said Anna Ebert, "is that what you have is no longer a legal problem, but a political problem. And I'm here to help you with the politics of it."

CHAPTER 11

Darlene Bundt dried the wineglasses that had come out
of the dishwasher behind the bar and slid them upside-
down into their slots in the hanging racks. She stretched
her slight frame to its utmost height to reach the upper
racks, jutting her tongue out of her mouth as she did so.
Her long bleach-blond hair fell back against her black-
lace cami top, revealing her multiple diamond ear studs.
She was thirty-five, but dressed as if she were twenty;
she could pull it off with her figure. Only the cruel
daylight revealed her true age in her face. She was about
to close down for the night. The last customer had been
chased out of Quinn's Pub and Grill at 2:00 a.m. sharp,
and she was itching to leave.

Mickey Quinn was in the back room, tallying up the
receipts for the night. "I'm going now!" called out
Darlene to the closed door. There was no answer. She
picked up her purse and slung it over her shoulder.

She left by the side door that opened onto the
parking lot. She headed for her car, a ten year old
Volkswagen. She got in behind the driver's wheel but
did not turn on the car. Instead, she opened her purse
and got out a joint and lit it up, inhaling deeply. She put
the key in the ignition so she could turn on the radio.
The dark night was peaceful with the pinpricks of stars
and the white moon overhead.

Suddenly, there was a tapping on her window.
Darlene jumped, and cupped the lit joint in her right

hand, burning her palm. "Shit!" she exclaimed. She squinted against the window to see who it was, then lowered it an inch to talk. Smoke leaked out.

"Gotcha," said Mickey Quinn, grinning. "Didn't know my new bartender liked the wacky weed."

"Jesus, Mr. Quinn, you scared the shit outta me."

"Why? Didja think I might be a cop?"

"I don't know. I just didn't expect anybody to come along just then."

"So what'll ya do for me for not calling the cops on you?"

"It's legal now in Massachusetts, Mr. Quinn."

"Not if a person's about to drive."

She sighed deeply. Her face sagged, as she suddenly looked her age. "Whaddya want from me, Mr. Quinn?"

Mickey Quinn grinned. The full moon shone directly over his head, making his eyes glitter. "Did I ever tell you you're a mighty good-looking woman?"

"I don't believe this," Darlene muttered to herself.

"I think a lady such as yourself, one who smokes the wacky weed, would be up for a little bit of fun now and then."

"What did you have in mind?"

"Why don't you step into my Cadillac, over there," he gestured across the parking lot, "and we'll talk about it."

"No thanks. I think I'll just get on home, now." Darlene turned off her radio, and turned her key further to start the ignition. It made a low, rasping noise, but the engine didn't start. "Shit!" she said again. She turned the ignition again, pumping harder on the gas, but the engine just made a rasping noise. "God damn it!" She whirled in her seat towards Mickey Quinn. "Did you do something to my car?" she asked.

"Getting paranoid, are you, from that wacky weed?"

"No, God damn it! My car was working just fine earlier today. Just seems damn peculiar, if you ask me." She pounded the dashboard in frustration.

"Need a ride home?"

Darlene sighed, sat motionless for a long moment, debating whether she could trust him, then decided she had little choice but to accept a ride from him in the middle of the night. She literally had no one she could call. She had no one but her grandmother, who was in a nursing home. Sighing again, she removed her key from the ignition, and got out of her car. She shut the driver's door and locked it. A lot of good that did her now, she thought.

"My chariot awaits." Mickey Quinn slipped his hand under her elbow and escorted her to his Cadillac. He hit a button on his key-ring and the locks sprung open. He opened the door to the passenger seat and said "Get in." She did.

"Now, he said. "How about sharing a bit of that wacky weed you've got burning a hole in your hand?"

"You're a fine one to talk about me smoking weed," Darlene said, pulling out her lighter for him.

Mickey Quinn just took a deep inhalation, held it, and then exhaled.

Darlene took another hit. "When are you driving me

home?"

"Soon. After a little of this," he said, as he suddenly leaned forward and kissed her full on the mouth.

"Jesus Christ! You're married!"

Mickey laughed. "Like that's ever stopped me?"

Darlene began shoving him back, and he leaned away for a moment towards the steering wheel. She couldn't see in the night-time shadows what he was doing. Then she realized he was opening his pants.

"Pull your jeans down, Darlene, or I'll turn the cops onto you."

"For what? For smokin' a joint? You're smokin' it, too! "

"Yeah, but I don't deal it, like you do."

Darlene began to think fast. Would Mickey Quinn really rat her out to the cops?

"Come on, Mickey," she coaxed. "You wouldn't really do that to me, would you?"

He smiled thinly in the moonlight. "Unlike you, I don't have two prior drug convictions. Third one, and it's mandatory jail time. But you know that already."

Darlene froze. How did he know?

As if reading her thoughts, he said, "Of course, I do a thorough background check on every employee I hire at my place. It helps that I'm friendly with several members on the police force who can look up prior convictions."

"Jesus, Mickey."

"A search of your place might turn up your stash."

"Why'd you even hire me, then?"

Mickey Quinn didn't answer her question. Instead,

he began tugging at the waistband of her jeans. He undid the middle button, unzipped the short zipper. He tugged the jeans downwards, till they started sliding down her thighs.

"Please, Mickey, let's not do this. Take me home. Just take me home."

"I even know who sells you weed, Darlene, and who you sell it to, afterwards. All I have to do is make a call to our local boys in blue. Whaddya say, Darlene?"

"Okay, Mickey," she whispered. "You got me."

"Atta girl." His smile glistened under the moonlight.

"Just make it quick."

"Pull down your jeans, Darlene." His voice took on an urgent tone, and he gripped her shoulder tightly.

Darlene sighed, and slipped off her jeans. Her panties followed.

Mickey was on her in a moment, his weight pressing her down into the leather upholstery of the car-seat, his smell of aftershave cologne, sweat, and marijuana-breath bearing down on her, to nearly smother her. His cheek stubble chafed against her forehead. It was over in a few minutes, when he groaned and lay slack upon her.

Darlene pushed him off her and raised herself upon her elbows. She reached for the front of Mickey's shirt and wiped herself down. Let him go home with that on his clothes, she thought. See if his wife notices.

Darlene sat up completely and pulled up her panties and jeans. She was going home, if she had to walk home. Diverse thoughts flashed through her mind in

67

rapid succession. Should she go to the hospital for a rape-testing? That would implicate Mickey Quinn, but, unfortunately, he was above the law. The D.A. would never go after him, she thought. Plus, if I even tried, he'd bring out my weed smoking and dealing. I can't face that hitting the fan.

Worse even, I still have to work for that bastard. I need my job, or I'll be out of my apartment, with nowhere to go, she thought. How can I face him again? Ever? With what he's done, with what he knows about me?

"Dreaming of me?" said Mickey Quinn softly, as he made a move to pull his pants up over his rear end.

"Hardly." said Darlene.

"Okay, babe, let me take you home so you can get some sleep. You're on tomorrow night, right?"

Darlene sighed heavily. She paused. "Yeah."

"See you then."

"Yeah."

Darlene was driven home within fifteen minutes. As soon as her key unlocked her apartment door, and she was inside, she began to shake uncontrollably. She felt cold, goose-fleshy, jumbled-up in her guts. She walked numbly to her bedroom, took off her clothes, dropped them on the floor as if they were contaminated, and then walked to the bathroom. She ran warm water in the bathtub till it was half full. She stepped into the water and sat down in the tub. She began to scrub herself down with soap and a loofah. When she had scrubbed every bit of herself, she finally lay back in the tub to let the water relax her. Tears began to well up behind her eyelids. The bastard. Well, she would never let him see that he had gotten the best of her. She'd get back at him somehow, someday. In the meantime, she'd have to go back to work tomorrow and act as if nothing at all had happened. She would be a god-damned stone-face about it all, and never let him have the satisfaction of knowing he had wounded her.

Meanwhile, in the Cadillac, Mickey Quinn had parked on a dead-end street of Longbottom. He turned off his engine, shut off his lights, and felt around on the floor of the car for the remainder of the joint. He turned his car key partially, to power up the car's cigarette lighter, to ignite the joint. As he smoked it, he felt an unaccustomed sense of euphoria and well-being. That Darlene was a hot little number. And this weed was good stuff.

Good stuff comes to those who help themselves, he mused. With that thought foremost in his mind, he snapped open the glove compartment. Carefully, he withdrew the distributor cap from the Volkswagen that he had pocketed much earlier in the evening. It was the "mysterious malfunction" that had led Darlene into his car and into his pants. It would have to be replaced, tonight, before she discovered it was missing. In the morning, her car would start up as usual, no doubt perplexing her, but she would be none the wiser. He chuckled to himself as he smoked the very last of the weed.

CHAPTER 12

"Just what did you mean by a political problem?" asked Maureen. "I'm afraid I don't get it." She leaned forward in her hard wooden chair to stare at Anna Ebert intently.

"What I propose is a political solution," said Anna. She planted her thin elbows on the edge of her huge desk which was covered with paperwork. "You see, the selectmen voting for eminent domain was a political action. We all know that it was a decision that favors Mickey Quinn's interests." She smiled ruefully. "At least, we suspect as much."

"Can we get the District Attorney to go after Mickey Quinn?" asked Robert.

"On what grounds? We have no proof of a conspiracy. Mere suspicion is not enough." Anna Ebert blinked hard for a long moment, sighed, and began again. "Our target right now is the *selectmen*, who performed a political act against you two."

Dust motes floated down from the ceiling, illuminated in the shaft of sunlight that came through the tall windows. Robert and Maureen remained silent and motionless, pondering Anna Ebert's words.

"You need to respond to the *selectmen*, in a *political manner*," she repeated.

"How?" asked Robert.

"By a recall election against all three of them."

"What?" said Robert and Maureen together.

"You heard me," said Anna Ebert, eyes twinkling.

"That should get their attention."

"I'd say," said Maureen with a quick, hoarse laugh.

Robert began a rumbling, belly-shaking chuckle. His coal-black eyes curled up at the corners, and he rubbed his hair, mussing it until it stuck out at odd angles. He was unabashedly entertained at the thought.

"The mere threat of a recall should get them to reverse their vote on the eminent domain," continued Anna. "You know how politicians hate to lose their public positions."

When Robert had stopped laughing, he said, "I can see how that would put the screws to them. They deserve it. But how do we do a recall election?"

"Is it even legal for us to do it?" interjected Maureen.

"Of course it is! This is America! Land of the Free, etc., etc.," said Anna Ebert. "Anyway, under our Open Town Meeting form of local government, there's a recall provision."

"Huh," said Maureen. "Who knew?"

"And it's available to ordinary citizens," added Anna Ebert helpfully.

"Somehow they didn't teach us that part in high school," said Robert.

"They wouldn't," Anna said. "But that's another discussion for another day. Don't get me started." She rolled her eyes towards the ceiling.

"Wait, tell us briefly what they left out in high school that we need to know," said Robert.

"You already know most of it," said Anna, "just by having gone to Open Town Meeting all these years. You know that town meeting is the legislative branch of local government, while the selectmen are the executive branch. You already know that the people of the town, who make up the members of an Open Town Meeting, are able to pass by-laws that govern the town. The state's attorney general has to approve the by-laws, but that's usually automatic. Some years ago, Longbottom passed a by-law to be able to recall elected officials. The selectmen opposed it, but it passed Town Meeting, and the attorney general approved it. So it's available to you, now that you need it."

"So, how do we do this thing?" asked Robert with a hint of impatience.

"First, you two have to get the recall petitions from the town clerk. He has them in his office, up at town hall. Second, you'd have to get signatures from registered voters in Longbottom on the petitions. You'd need two hundred signatures on the petitions. Third, you'd turn in the petitions to the town clerk, and he'd have to call the special recall election within sixty days. If a majority of the people voting in the election voted to recall them, they'd be out of office."

"Seems like a big undertaking," said Maureen.

"It is," admitted Anna. "But it's the only way I see for you to get the eminent domain reversed. Either they'll reverse it before the recall election, for fear of the consequences, or they'll tough it out and we'll just have to vote them out of office."

"There's no other way, huh?" asked Robert, no longer chuckling.

"No," said Anna. "You'll lose in court. All the

courts are bound, hand and foot, by the deciding case of *Kelo*. No judge will go against the U.S. Supreme Court."

"I guess that's it, then," said Robert, clapping his hands on his knees as he sat. "We're gonna hafta turn ourselves into a bunch of politicians."

"You are," said Anna.

"This thing is gonna hit the town like a tornado," said Robert.

Anna Ebert grinned. "It'll do the town good, bring 'em up into the twenty-first century. It's about time."

"Mind if I ask you a personal question, Attorney Ebert?" asked Maureen.

"Sure." Anna Ebert's green eyes were calm but alert.

"Why are you willing to go against the political establishment in this town? Every other lawyer we talked to is terrified of taking our case. They're all afraid of Mickey Quinn's involvement, and Tobias Meachum, too."

Anna Ebert sighed. "I wouldn't be much of a lawyer if I were afraid, would I?" She flexed her slender neck from side to side. "It's a long story, really. But I can give you a brief synopsis of it, I guess." She folded her hands on the edge of her desk. "You know my mom and my dad, the Eberts, who live out on Liberty Lane, off of Grand Avenue?"

"Yep," said Robert. "Your dad taught math up at the high school."

"That's right, he did. For a while. At least until Mickey Quinn had him fired for suspending some boys who came to school with liquor and drugs. When the principal asked them where they had gotten the stuff, one of them had named Quinn's Pub and Grill, Mickey Quinn's place. My dad suggested reporting this fact to the DA's office. The principal must've let Mickey know about my father's idea, because the next thing he knew, Mickey Quinn was calling for his, my dad's, immediate resignation."

"On what grounds?" asked Maureen.

"On the grounds that my father had searched their lockers without permission and without calling for a police officer to do it instead. Mickey Quinn said my dad had violated their civil rights." She snorted derisively. "Mickey Quinn, the protector of civil liberties."

"So what happened?" asked Maureen.

"My dad soon found it impossible to work there. The harassment was subtle but real. He ended up quitting. He never went back to teaching. He has a home business, repairing antique clocks."

"I'm sorry," said Maureen. "I didn't realize he had touched your family adversely, too." Her gray-blue eyes had clouded over. She pursed her lips slightly. "So you've been waiting for a case like this, haven't you?" she said softly.

Anna Ebert nodded slightly. Her green eyes gleamed. "It's been a long wait."

"How long have you been a lawyer?" asked Maureen.

"Ten years," said Anna. "I'm older than I look. Still unmarried, too, to my mother's chagrin."

"Don't worry, you've still got time," said Maureen

soothingly.

"Not much, to hear my mother. But that's another story." She looked at the five-and-dime-clock on the far wall and saw it was noon. Time for lunch." Anna glanced over her shoulder to look out the window. The leafy Linden tree swayed in a sudden gust of wind. "Looks like it's clouded over while we've talked. Wonder if we're going to get one of those summer storms this afternoon."

"We've kept you here too long," said Maureen.

"Don't be silly. It was well-spent getting to know one another a bit. Actually, I want you two to come back tomorrow, too. We'll go to town hall together to get those recall petitions started. Mustn't waste time getting started!"

CHAPTER 13

Clarisse lay awake at 4:00 a.m. on her satin sheets, on her king-size bed, wondering where Mickey was at that hour. The grey light of the television flickered unevenly across her face and jumbled hair. She punched her feather pillow to make a hollow for her head, then punched the pillow a few more times in agitation.

Clarisse willed herself to dwell on happy scenes from her childhood, such as summers spent around the campfire in her parents' backyard, roasting marshmallows with friends, and laughing at ghost stories that were supposed to be scary. She forced her eyelids shut until they burned with the unnatural pressure and they flew open again. *Where was he?*

The automatic garage door opening brought some instant relief.

That sound was followed by that of the Cadillac engine entering the garage, then being shut off. She heard the garage door close. A car door slammed. The door from the garage to the house was softly opened and shut. Footsteps padded up the stairs to their second floor bedroom. Clarisse shut her eyes and feigned sleep. The handle turned and the door swung open.

Mickey softly walked into the bedroom. First he shut off the television. The bedroom became murky in the darkness but for a sliver of moonlight peeping in through the drawn curtains. His breathing seemed loud in the sudden silence of no TV.

76

He took off his clothes and draped them over the back of a chair. He sat on the edge of the bed then stripped off his boxer briefs and let them drop to the floor beside the bed.

Then he lay back in bed on top of the covers. *He reeks of marijuana smoke*, thought Clarisse. *Since when has he taken that up? I knew he liked his beer, and his scotch, but this? This is new. Hmm.*

Eventually, Mickey's loud breathing became steadier and he relaxed into sleep. Clarisse let herself relax, too, knowing that he was home, and not dead out on the highway. Finally, she slept.

At 10:00 a.m., Clarisse woke up, heavy-limbed, and burning-eyed. Her memory of the previous night struck her like a bolt of lightning. She sat up, ready to find out what she could. Mickey was still fast asleep, sprawled across two-thirds of the bed. Clarisse tiptoed over to Mickey's side of the bed and picked up his clothes. She made no noise on the cream-colored wall-to-wall carpeting in the bedroom. She put the clothes in the laundry basket that lay on the floor near the room-length closets opposite their bed. She intended to examine the clothing more closely, later.

Clarisse glanced back over at her husband. He still slept without a care in the world. His light-brown, golden-tinged hair fell back from his forehead in a tumble, and he looked younger than his years with his eyes closed. When he slept, the shrewd expression, the air of perpetual amusement, was gone. His persona was his offensive move she realized. He charmed people until they didn't know which way was up.

He certainly charmed me into marrying him, she thought. Would I have married him if I had really known him? That was a question she couldn't answer yet.

Clarisse lifted the laundry basket and carried it out of the bedroom. She could do her sleuthing in the laundry room, where Mickey would never suspect. She proceeded with the basket down the stairs to the first floor, then down another set of stairs to the basement laundry room. She pulled the chain to turn on the bare light bulb over the washer and dryer. She spilled out the laundry on top of the washing machine. First, she picked up Mickey's pants and felt in all the pockets. She was searching for a slip of paper with a phone number on it, or a card with a woman's name. There was nothing but stray coins in his right front pocket. Next she checked his shirt. She checked the breast pocket. Nothing. She checked the collar for signs of lipstick. Nothing. She was going to toss the shirt into the front-loading washing machine when she felt a crusty, stiff patch on the front waist and side of the shirt. She held it up to the light. She didn't see anything, but now that she held it closer to her face, she distinctly caught the smell of sex. Somebody had wiped themselves with Mickey's shirt after sex.

She knew it. He was a cheater. He had cheated with some marijuana-smoking woman who had kept him out late last night.

She felt hollow-sick and hurt-angry, all at the same time. What was she going to do about it? she wondered. Hmm. The only advantage I have, is that he doesn't know that I know, yet. Let's see how he acts towards me, she thought. I'll be able to read his expression over the morning coffee. Which we'll probably have after noontime because he was out so late. Let's see if he tries to bluff his way out of this one!

CHAPTER 14

Anna Ebert and the Jastons stood outside of town hall on a sparkling, sunny, June morning. Town hall stood to one side of the oval town common, which was lushly green in the shade of the many flowering trees. The building itself was a tall, two-story wooden structure built in the 1800s and painted white. Just inside the heavy double doors was the office of town clerk. Anna and the Jastons had been gathered on the sidewalk for a good ten minutes or so, summoning the will to start their plans.

"So, are we ready to go into the lion's den?" Though it was hot, Anna looked unflappable in her cream-colored linen suit and ice-blue blouse.

"Ready if you are," said Maureen.

The three walked up the steps to the entryway. Robert held the heavy door for the women then followed them inside. They stopped at the window counter of the town clerk. A young woman sat typing at a computer. The town clerk sat, back to the window counter and feet up on his desk, chatting on his cell phone. Neither seemed inclined to help them.

"Ahem," said Anna, loudly.

After a long moment, the young woman looked up. "How can I help you?"

"We're here to begin a recall petition on each of the three selectmen," said Anna Ebert.

There was a long silence while the young woman

absorbed what had been said. Then she turned away from the counter and went over to the town clerk to get his attention.

The town clerk, Rufus Fishbane, was in the middle of telling a joke and laughing. He waved the young woman away.

The young woman pursed her lips and tried again. "Rufus," she whispered loudly. "I need your help!"

"Okay, John, I'll catch you later..." Rufus said, before closing his cell phone.

"Geeze, Sally! You saw I was on the phone."

Sally pointed to the people waiting behind his back. Rufus Fishbane swung his feet down off his desk with a thump and swiveled around. "Hello, folks! I'll just be a second." He picked up a pad of paper and pen and brought them to the window counter.

"What can we do for you?"

"We're here to start some recall petitions on each of the three selectmen," Anna announced.

"What?" he exclaimed. "You gotta be kiddin' me!"

"We're not," said Anna. "Though we know you like jokes."

"Well, the whole idea is a sick joke!"

"Hardly," said Anna. "How about rustlin' up some petitions, cowboy?"

Rufus Fishbane's face, which was framed by dark, graying hair and a graying beard, turned purplish-red with rage. He was a thin, tall man, and he bent lower to put his face even with Anna Ebert's. "Now, listen, little lawyer-lady: you tell your clients here to quit their foolishness and go home before they stir up a hornet's nest."

"I will do no such thing, Rufus Fishbane!" exclaimed Anna Ebert. "Now you look here: You draw up those recall petitions, right now, or I will march into court and get a mandatory injunction on you forcing you to do it!"

Anna Ebert, all five-foot-two-inches of her, stared hard into Rufus Fishbane's angry dark brown eyes until he blinked and looked down at the counter. He turned around to Sally who had been standing by, helplessly, holding a sheaf of papers.

"Here's the forms, Mr. Fishbane," said Sally.

"Thanks, Sally. Okay. I'll write the lead paragraph," he said. "When I'm done, you can type up the forms." He went to his desk, bent over the recall forms and the recall by-law, then began to write on his yellow pad. After a few minutes, he handed the yellow pad to Sally. "Here, type this up, with signature lines at the bottom of the page."

Sally sat at her computer and began to type. When she was done, she stood to print out a copy. She handed it to Rufus, who handed it to Anna.

Anna looked at the document briefly. "Rufus, you know this is no good."

"Whaddya mean? It names all three selectmen, just like you asked me to."

"I asked for petitions for all three selectmen. Not for all three selectmen to be on a single petition. You know very well each person has to have his or her own petition."

"I don't know that that's required."

"Come on, Rufus. You're town clerk. You ought to know it. Either you're stupid or you're being devious."

"Insulting me won't help you."

"Maybe suing you would."

Rufus gave Anna another evil look but got his yellow pad and began to rewrite the petitions. After a minute he handed Sally an amended form to type, which she began immediately.

Robert and Maureen hadn't said a word throughout this exchange, but at this point they glanced at one another, encouraged. They flanked little Anna Ebert like her bodyguards, or witnesses, and marveled at her determination.

When Sally was finished, she printed out all three petitions, one after the other. She handed all three to Rufus.

Anna looked them over carefully. When she was satisfied, she said, "Okay, make us thirty copies of each petition, and then we'll be on our way."

"You have to get two hundred signatures on each petition," said Rufus. "You'll never get people in this town to agree to sign." He snickered. "And if anyone signs improperly, their signature will be invalidated. By me."

"We'll see you when the petitions are filled with signatures, Rufus," said Anna. "I'm sure you'll be waiting for us with bells on your toes!"

With that, she whirled around on one shoe and began the trek out of town hall. The Jastons followed, amazed.

CHAPTER 15

"So who's going to be our supporters in this petition drive?" asked Maureen on the drive home from town hall.

Robert didn't answer immediately, but frowned over the steering wheel of the red Ford truck. "I guess I can call up some of my buddies," he said after a pause. "Maybe Tim and Ron and Rick will do it. Maybe their wives will help us out."

"We'll make some calls as soon as we get home," suggested Maureen. "I'll get out the Christmas card list and get names off of that."

Mr. James Rutherford was the first to answer the call to arms. Next was Joe Ferrer, a long-time friend to Robert's now-deceased father. Also joining were Tim, Ron, Rick, and a few others who Robert had known growing up in Longbottom Also joining the small army of well-wishers-and-petitioners were Maureen's friends, Dee Glasson and Sue Nevins, who had been Maureen's new-found friends in high school.

Two days later, at seven in the evening, a string of cars gathered in the curved gravel driveway of the Jaston farm. A few early stars were out and could be seen through the trees lining the driveway. The birds settling in for the evening were chattering and calling to one another. At the top of the driveway, the windows of the Jaston farmhouse reflected the brilliance of the fiery sunset.

The group of people found themselves in the front room of the farmhouse, with its formal couch and chairs. The room was infrequently used and had an old-fashioned, static quality to it, with out-of-date wall paper and lace doilies covering the end tables.

Extra chairs had been brought in from the kitchen to accommodate the crowd. Maureen served coffee and cake.

"Welcome, everyone," said Robert. "Thank you for coming to help us. As you know, Maureen and I are in serious trouble over this eminent domain situation. We've brought our lawyer, Anna Ebert, to this meeting to explain what needs to be done."

Anna stood up to face the assembly. "Some of you may know my parents, Paul and Dorothy Ebert. My father has a clock repair business over on Liberty Lane, and my mother is a secretary at Connor Real Estate."

"What time is it, now?" joked Tim.

"Time to help your friends," answered Anna smoothly.

"Stow it, Tim," said Mr. Rutherford.

"Do people know what to do?" asked Anna Ebert. She looked over at Robert and Maureen. "You have to go out and get signatures on the petitions. That's easy enough, right? Just make sure that people sign with their legal name."

"How do we do that?" asked Rick.

"Most people will sign their legal names without a problem. But you don't want anyone signing 'Mickey Mouse' instead of their name, that kind of thing," said Anna.

"Seems simple enough," said Mr. Rutherford, rubbing his sore knees.

"Do people know where to go?" asked Anna Ebert.

"The supermarket, the hardware store, the coffee shops, the town dump, the post office, and church," said Dee.

"You're right about everything except the post office. The post office doesn't allow any political activity on its premises or its grounds," said Anna. "Everyplace else is great."

"Especially church," laughed Sue.

Anna Ebert grinned. "Churches have a long history of political movements. Think of the abolitionist movement. Think of the civil rights movement. There's a great precedent for bringing petitions to church."

"We're hardly civil rights workers," said Sue, rolling her eyes, expecting the group to laugh with her. No one responded.

Anna went on. "You definitely should think of yourselves as civil rights workers. As I see it, this abuse of eminent domain is, indeed, a civil rights issue. People should have a right to the quiet enjoyment of their property without the threat of politicians arbitrarily assigning it to someone who has more money and political clout."

She stopped, aware that her tone was growing heated, and attempted a smile.

"But what the selectmen did is legal, isn't it?" asked Mr. Rutherford.

"Yes, unfortunately, it is," admitted Anna. "That doesn't make it right. And these petitions are about it being 'not right'."

"How is it legal?" asked Mr. Rutherford.

"By a deciding case of the U.S. Supreme Court," said Anna.

"Doesn't that mean it's all over? The issue is decided?" asked Mr. Rutherford.

Anna smiled a tight-lipped smile and said, "Not necessarily. The U.S. Supreme Court hasn't always been right, you know. What about the infamous Dred Scott case, where the Supreme Court decided slavery was legal? That was hardly a stellar moment of the Court. Ultimately, the Court was proved wrong by the Civil War."

"Well, I don't see how the comparison is relevant. We're hardly going to enter into a Civil War over this," said Sue, rolling her eyes again.

"No, but if citizens all over the country start making the political climate tough for their elected officials on this eminent domain issue, eventually, change will come. From the bottom up. That's how real political change usually happens, anyway," said Anna. "And we're here, in our little corner of the country, to make our own elected officials very uncomfortable on this issue."

"We know it's the right thing to do," chimed in Maureen.

"This is my only option," interjected Robert Jaston. "I have no choice."

"I'm in, my boy," said Mr. Rutherford. "I knew your father, and he'd be sick at heart to know that the selectmen of the town he loved had turned against his farm. How about the rest of you?"

A chorus of "Me, too!" arose from the assembly in the Jastons' front room.

"Then each of you take two copies of the petition, and get them completely filled with signatures," said Anna Ebert. "Have all twenty-five lines filled on both pages, agreed? And then we'll meet back here, same time, two weeks from today."

CHAPTER 16

Maureen Jaston was in a hurry. She had to prepare a quick dinner for her family before the crowd of their supporters descended upon their farmhouse. Once again she was making a large, dozen-egg omelet for the five of them for their dinner. Her cooking had gotten noticeably skimpier ever since they had started the recall petition process.

She and Robert, along with their three children, ate quickly, barely talking.

The family tradition of sitting and eating in a leisurely way, and encouraging thoughtful discussions with their children, had fallen by the wayside. The only family talk there was these days was of politics.

The first of their supporters began arriving while Maureen was still washing the dishes.

Dee Glasson was at the kitchen door, with Sue Nevins close behind her. The setting sun glowed over the treetops behind their heads, and the summer air was humid and fragrant with flowers.

"Come in! Come in!" exclaimed Maureen. "Great to see you both!"

"We got our petitions completely filled!" said Dee.

"Great! We'll have to see how the others did, too."

As they spoke, other supporters began arriving, entering by the kitchen door, rather than the formal, little-used front entrance. The chattering voices raised in volume.

89

Maureen busily poured coffee into cups and lined them up on the kitchen table.

People began adding their own cream and sugar, then carrying their coffee to the formal sitting room, where the meeting would be held.

Anna Ebert arrived to a flurry of voices. "Come, everyone! Let's get this meeting started," she called out gently. "So, how did everybody do?"

"Pretty good!" one man called out.

"Filled 'er all up!" exclaimed another.

"Well done, everyone! Tomorrow morning, the Jastons and I will take these petitions to town hall, to the office of Rufus Fishbane. We'll get him to certify the signatures and officially register the recall petitions for a recall election."

She pivoted from one side of the crowd to the other side in order to make eye contact with everyone in the room. She cracked open a wide grin. "That oughta be a real fun time."

The room burst into laughter then excited talking.

Anna resumed, "We'll keep you all informed as to how it goes. If the newspapers don't scoop us."

***

Anna and the Jastons drove over to town hall in the Jastons' truck. They had made a prior stop at the copying center, to make multiple copies of the many-paged petitions. They left the copies in the truck cab and locked it.

Anna was carrying the three separate, original

petitions, along with a copy of each one, in a manila folder.

As they got out of the truck, they looked around the town common to see if anyone was around. No doubt, news of their storming town hall with the petitions would fly all over town in a matter of minutes.

"I feel like an old cowhand taking on the corrupt town boss," commented Robert. "This moment feels surreal."

"It's all too real, honey," said Maureen softly, coming up beside him.

"Let's go," said Anna. "And don't sweat it; Rufus has got no choice." She stood on the first of the granite steps leading up to the town hall, turned, and went up to the heavy, glass front door.

Robert hastily moved forward to open it for her and Maureen.

The three of them walked a short distance down the hallway to the town clerk's office.

"Ruuuufus!" called out Anna sarcastically. "Where are you?"

Rufus poked his head out around the corner and came forward to the front counter. His face was reddish-purple with suppressed rage. "What do you want?"

"We're here to file our recall petitions with you, and to have them date/time stamped as proof of our having filed them," said Anna. "It'll only take you a moment, then we can be on our way while you go about the business of checking all the names."

Rufus Fishbane scowled. He reached for the date/time stamp of the Town of Longbottom, and began stamping each page savagely. There were more than fifty pages in all, and he pounded away at page after page. At last he was done.

"Now the same for our copies of the petitions, Rufus," said Anna.

He glared at her but said nothing. He reached for the second sheaf of papers and began stamping away at each page. After a long several minutes he was done.

"Thank you, Rufus. Now that wasn't so painful, was it?"

Rufus turned away from Anna and the Jastons without answering.

He tossed the pile of original petitions on the desk of his assistant, Sally, and said, "Go through those petitions and check every name. If a name isn't signed exactly the way the person registered to vote, then disallow the name." He turned to eye the trio. "When we get done, we'll see if you still have enough legitimate signatures to get this recall election started."

"I have no doubt we'll be fine, Rufus. We have double and triple the number of necessary signatures."

"We'll see," said Rufus ominously.

"Yes, we will. And don't forget: I won't hesitate to report you to the necessary state officials if you obstruct us. Or to sue you for a mandatory injunction to hold the recall election. It's your choice ultimately."

Anna turned to the Jastons. "Let's go; we won't find any friends here!"

So they left town hall, piled into the truck, and went for lunch at a restaurant in the next town, Orangeville.

CHAPTER 17

Two days later, Anna was working late at her office. She was thinking hard about the Jaston case and wondering how they could pull off a win in the court of public opinion. There had to be a way to get the word out to the ordinary voter about the essential injustice at the heart of this matter.

The recall election would be coming in another ten weeks or so, just as soon as the petition signatures were certified and a slate of replacement candidates filed their nomination papers. That was another problem: Who was going to be on their slate of replacement candidates? One problem at a time, she decided.

Suddenly, Anna had a brilliant idea. She picked up the phone and called her friend, Sophie Parson. "Sophie, can you come to my office today after work? I have an interesting proposition for you."

"What's it about, Anna?"

"I'll tell you in person." Anna put the phone back in its cradle and laughed aloud. Sophie was an artist for a t-shirt company, designing logos, images, and such. This was going to be good.

Promptly at 4:30, Sophie pulled into a parking space in front of Anna's law office. Sophie was a big woman, nearly 5'10', with flaming red hair and blazing blue eyes. She and tiny, dark, Anna Ebert, were an eye-catching contrast in opposites when they stood together. Nevertheless, they had been friends since elementary school, despite all the disparaging comments about how they looked so strange together. These days, they reveled in it.

Sophie bounded up the shabby, carpeted steps to Anna's office, curiosity driving her forward. She burst into Trudy's front office, breathing hard. "Hi, Trudy. Anna in?"

"She's waiting for you. Last client left forty-five minutes ago. Go on in."

Sophie swung open the door to Anna's office, arms outstretched. Anna stood up behind her desk and came around to the front to hug Sophie fiercely. They exclaimed over each other, looked each other over again, then hugged once more.

"It's been too long," said Sophie. "How long has it been?"

"Maybe five or six months," said Anna. "Ridiculous, really, when we only live two towns away from each other. How is Jeffrey?"

"He's great. I married a sweetheart."

"Great," said Anna. "Now find me one."

"You've already rejected all of Jeffrey's friends. I don't have an infinite supply."

"Why not?"

"What am I? The computer of E-Harmony?"

"Don't talk to me about computer dating. I have the worst story for you."

"What?"

"It'll have to wait. Today is business."

"I'm dying to know."

"Think about what I'm going to propose as a

career-stretcher."

"Uh-oh. Now I'm in for it," said Sophie, only half-jokingly.

"Don't say no 'til you've heard me out completely. Well, have you heard about the Jaston farm and the selectmen of Longbottom taking it away from the them by eminent domain?"

"I thought I heard some rumors about that over in my town."

"I represent the Jastons as their lawyer. Well, we're organizing a recall against the selectmen."

"Ha!" shouted Sophie. She laughed. Her red hair flounced on her head, her normally pale complexion turned pink, and she jiggled in her chair. "Go get 'em, girl!"

"Good! Then you approve."

"Sure do." Sophie continued to giggle.

"You, as an artist, have a unique contribution to make to the cause."

"How's that?" asked Sophie, abruptly ceasing to giggle.

"You can draw political cartoons of the situation and submit them to the Longbottom Tribune. I already know they'll publish them. I've spoken to their editor, Steve Ballast, who says he considers political cartoons to be another form of editorial. I've represented him on a few minor matters, and he's open to suggestions. In the meantime, he's looking for something to spice up his paper and boost circulation."

"What? Are you crazy?" exclaimed Sophie, openmouthed.

"Why not?" asked Anna. She tapped her pencil eraser against the wooden surface of her desk methodically.

"What do I know about political cartoons?"

"What's so hard? Turn to me for the latest political developments, and draw a picture of it."

"I can draw, certainly," Sophie mused. "But what do I draw pictures of?"

"Caricatures of the selectmen with the latest outrageous thing they've said. People will be appalled when they see what comes out of their mouths in print."

"But I don't know the details of what they've said. Since I don't live in town, I don't get your cable television coverage of the selectmen's meetings."

"Don't worry. I've got a list here with some choice quotes."

Anna watched as Sophie fell silent, contemplating the matter. Anna could almost watch Sophie's thoughts as they flitted across her face. Doubt, confusion, excitement, determination.

"You know they say a picture is worth a thousand words," Anna added in a low voice.

Sophie's blue eyes blazed forth. "Will I have to put my name on the cartoons?"

"Yes."

The blue light in Sophie's eyes wavered.

"This calls for a certain amount of bravery on your part. But think of it as a potential new profession, political cartooning. Do you really want to design t-shirts your whole life?"

"No, that's for sure." Sophie sighed heavily.

"Against my better judgment, I'll do it for you, Anna."

"Thanks."

"But if I get sued, I'll need you to defend me. For free. I can't afford a legal defense."

"I will. I promise."

"Thank you," said Sophie. "Now where is that list of selectmen stupid quotes?"

"I've got a copy right here in my desk," said Anna, smiling. "I look forward to your first creation."

CHAPTER 18

Darlene Bundt knew she was pregnant. She could feel it. Her breasts felt tender and her pelvis felt bloated. It was horrible, someone her age, getting pregnant from unprotected, nonconsensual sex, but so it was. And there she was, faced with an unwelcome decision. Have the baby or not?

Darlene didn't relish telling Mickey about the baby because that just brought up the whole tawdry blackmail-rape situation. She had returned to bartending at Quinn's Pub afterwards, and Mickey had acted as if nothing had occurred between them. Two could play that game, she had thought, and she had acted the same for several weeks, pointedly avoiding him.

But with the onset of symptoms, reality had intruded. She had decided today that she had to find out if she was really pregnant.

Before her shift she had driven over to the next town's pharmacy to buy a home pregnancy kit. She had raced back to her apartment, even driving through a red light, in her hurry to get to her bathroom, where she could pee on a stick and wait for the results. Of course the red plus sign showed up. As if she was surprised.

Darlene stretched upwards to reach the overhead wineglass rack, and put away the wineglasses she had just taken out of the dishwasher and hand-dried. Her long, blonde hair swung down into the small of her arched back. As she finished, her eyes flashed to the mirror behind the bar, and she caught the image of Mickey Quinn staring at her.

Fancy, the Devil himself is interested, she told herself. Well, soon enough, the day of reckoning would come. She turned away from the mirror and busied herself amongst the coolers of ice and bottles of beer. She refilled the dishes of beer-nuts and pretzels. She cleaned the blenders. Anything to avoid exchanging pleasantries with him.

Mickey was now seated at his usual corner table, his back to the wall, where he could see all who entered. The town lawyer, Tobias Meachum, sat askew in a chair at the end of the table. He was chewing on his fingernails and spitting out the clippings on the floor, much to Mickey's annoyance.

"I oughta get you a spittoon, like they got out West," offered Mickey.

"Maybe just a nail clipper, for Christmas," said Denton Clay in a feeble jest.

He made up the rest of the party at the table.

Mickey turned his head slowly to glare at him. "It's summer now. We'll be knee-deep in fingernails by Christmas. Unless you care to buy a broom."

Denton ducked his head of white, fly-blown hair slightly, then said, "I can clean up. I know how to handle a mess."

"I wonder," said Mickey.

"What's that supposed to mean?" asked Denton indignantly.

"Where were you on the Jaston matter?"

"I can still help. On the financing part, later."

"We'll see."

Denton was there yet again at the behest of Mickey Quinn. The latter was not going to let him off so easy, despite the alternate solution of the eminent domain taking place.

Mickey expected Denton to provide material support in some way for the project, although he had not to date specified how.

Denton was growing mighty tired of being summoned to Quinn's Pub on the flimsiest of pretexts.

"Well, if nothing's doing at the moment, can I go?" asked Denton. "I need to get back to the bank. This has been an over-generous lunch-hour as it is."

"We'll be in touch," Mickey reminded him.

"No doubt," murmured Denton as he stood up.

"Little cockamamie banker thinks he knows it all," rasped Tobias, when Denton had left the table. "Why doesn't he get a decent haircut?"

"Let's not quibble about grooming, shall we?" said Mickey. "And didn't you say you had to be back in court this afternoon?"

"Yeah, the court session begins again at two o'clock. I'd better get downtown."

Tobias gulped down his bourbon and water, picked up his briefcase, and strode out the door.

Mickey turned back to contemplate Darlene. He sensed something was up. He made a mental note to call her into his office later in the day. Yet as he slyly observed her, nothing was obvious. He shook his head, to himself.

Darlene felt the weight of her breasts in her

brassiere and now knew that what she felt was not imagined. The heaviness in her pelvis was slowing her down in her dance behind the bar. She wondered if she was responding to customers a bit more slowly and if they were tipping her a little less. She'd know if it were true at the end of the day. Surely she wasn't turning into the stereotypical pregnant woman already, full of hormonal changes and moods? That couldn't be.

The evening went by slowly. There were few customers, only the regulars, who were confirmed alcoholics in her book. She wondered why some of these people simply didn't go home. Surely it was more comfortable at home than being perched on a bar- stool.

At last the evening came to a close. The final customer was shooed out, and the clean-up began. Darlene was done in record time. As she picked up her purse to leave, Mickey called out to her, "Darlene, c'mere!"

Reluctantly, Darlene went into his back office.

"Shut the door, Darlene."

"I prefer it open, considering."

"When you hear what I'm gonna say, you'll prefer it closed." Mickey's clear blue eyes were penetrating, his golden hair fell gracefully over his forehead.

Darlene slowly closed the door behind her, but stood next to it, wary.

"Look, Darlene. We got off to a bad start. I like you. Very much. I'd like it if we had a little thing going on the side."

"You're kidding." Darlene felt her face redden.

"No, I'm not. Why do you say that?"

"Because you pretty much raped me, after you threatened me, don't you remember?" Darlene felt a cold rage begin to rise in her chest.

"I don't remember it that way at all. I just used my powers of persuasion, as I see it."

"Your powers of persuasion, as you call it, amount to blackmailing me to have sex with you. You told me you'd set the cops on me, or else. What was I supposed to do? Refuse you and then wait for my arrest?"

"Darlene, Darlene, you're blowing everything out of proportion. I wouldn't have done all that. I just said that stuff 'cause I wanted you so bad. I guess that makes me a cad, and for that I'm sorry."

"I can't believe I'm actually hearing Michael Quinn tell me that he's sorry. I should get a recording of that for posterity." Darlene's eyes were narrowed.

"So what do you say, huh?"

"I say forget it!"

"I can make it worth your while. I can give you a good raise, help you pay your rent."

"Great! Pay me; make me a whore!"

"You don't have to put it in those terms."

"Why not? It'd be the truth, wouldn't it?"

"Would it? The truth is all relative," said Mickey.

"You wanna know the truth? The real truth? The truth is that I'm pregnant, with your baby. I know it's yours 'cause I hadn't had sex with anyone in a long time. And I'm probably gonna have an abortion. So there."

Darlene turned and marched out of the office, leaving a stunned, suddenly speechless Mickey Quinn behind to contemplate the situation.

That ought to fix the high and mighty Mickey Quinn, thought Darlene with some satisfaction.

She marched out of Quinn's Pub into the parking lot and got into her Volkswagen to drive home. She drove intensely, glaring fiercely onward into the silvery arcs under the streetlights and the shadows surrounding their perimeters. She passed repeatedly through light and shadow on her way home until she reached the oasis of her apartment, which was vaguely lit from within. Soon she would rest in the golden glow of her little lamp on the night table by her bedside. And place her hands on her still-flat belly, while keeping her thoughts in limbo.

If only she could have seen Mickey Quinn back in his office just then. She would have seen a man with warm rivulets of salty tears running down his ruddy cheeks, shoulders hunched and heaving, liquid droplets falling silently onto the papers strewn across his desk.

CHAPTER 19

Sophie Parsons spread her sketchpad and pens out across her wooden dining table. Anna Ebert had been pestering her for a political cartoon to put in the local newspaper to help the Jastons. Sophie had been mulling over a series of images in her mind. She had decided on an office setting, with the selectmen's three heads and torsos lined up behind a desk. While she pondered the images, she sipped on her cup of tea.

As she began sketching, Sophie realized the images would have to be mere outlines. She would not be able to incorporate shading and other details into the drawings. In fact, she would be best off with caricature-like images. She would have to think of some outrageous statement each of them had made recently, to put into a bubble over their heads.

Sophie decided to start with Marilyn Hardy. She was tricky to draw. With her prim and proper schoolmarmish ways, she was plain-looking. There was nothing in her appearance to exaggerate. Sophie decided to draw her personality, rather than her physical traits. She would draw a woman with her nose up in the air, a sign of disapproval of others. Sophie drew her head with wavy hair around it, and a long, pointed nose angled upward. She drew beady eyes, wispy eyebrows, and a pursed mouth to complete the picture. Sophie laughed aloud at the picture. Now for the quotation in the bubble.

"That land is wasted with nothing but cows on it!"

Sophie intoned mock-seriously. She penned it in over the caricature of Marilyn Hardy.

When it was done, she smiled, satisfied. She leaned back in her chair to rest a moment then leaned forward to reach for her now cold cup of tea. The cold tea tasted more flavorful, and she didn't mind it.

"Onward," Sophie reminded herself. She picked up her pen and began to draw a caricature of Gerald Hopper. She drew his face a little beefier than it was in real life, to make him look like a well-fed country club member. Sophie concentrated on drawing the lines of his blown-back hair. She put him in a skin-tight polo shirt to make him look like a playboy. She put a smug smile on his face.

She put down her pen. She was satisfied with the image, but what was a pithy thing for him to say that was outrageous?

Sophie swiveled in her chair and rose to go to the hutch where she kept important papers. Anna had gotten her a transcript of the selectman's meeting where they had voted to invoke the eminent domain. She would have to pore over the transcript to find something he had said. Here was something ridiculous..."We act in the best interests of the town!"

"That's a laugh," said Sophie to herself. She sat back down in her chair and began to ink the quote into the bubble above his head. It looked satisfactorily ludicrous above his image.

When she was done, she rose again and went into the kitchen to make a fresh cup of tea. She added a teaspoon of sugar and a dollop of lemon juice and stirred it.

Sophie was feeling tired. And the hot tea was soothing. She didn't feel like completing the political cartoon, but she knew that if she quit now, her momentum would be lost. Reluctantly, she put her half-finished cup of tea down, and began the task of drawing Danny Tripiano.

At least he was easy. He was almost a caricature already. She decided to draw him in profile. It was his profile that was so amusing. His large hooked nose was easy to draw. Then there were his fleshy lips over a receding chin. There was also the little flat spot on the back of his head where he was bald. He had flashing dark eyes that were unusually large and round. Everything about his face was ripe for a caricature. Sophie chuckled as she drew him. He was almost too easy. He would be recognizable from this image if it hit the newspaper.

But what should she have him say?

Then it hit her. His constant statement at town meetings was: "Longbottom needs MORE money!" That would be the quote in the bubble above his head. Everyone in town would immediately recognize him for saying it.

The first political cartoon was done. It was pretty savage in its way, especially how it lampooned their physical appearances. On the other hand, what they were doing to the Jastons was savage, too. She would take it over to Anna in the morning to see what she thought. This would set the tongues of Longbottom wagging, no doubt.

CHAPTER 20

Darlene pulled the heavy wooden door of Quinn's Pub open and stepped into the dim, neon-lit interior. She felt sick to her stomach again. What was supposed to be just morning sickness was lasting well into the afternoons. She ran her fingers through her long, blonde hair to soothe herself, but her fingers became tangled in the windblown knots. Her life had become one big tangle.

"Darlene," called out Mickey from across the room. "I want to see you for a minute. Come into my office before you do your set-up." He rose from his corner booth in the back and went to his office to wait for her.

"Great. Just great," muttered Darlene. "What now?" She threaded her way through the tables and chairs, careful not to bump any. She felt that if she bumped anything it would upset her delicate balance of the moment. She eased to the office door sideways and poked her head around the door.

"Come in, come in," said Mickey, while seated behind his desk. "I won't bite." He waved his right arm in a welcoming manner.

"We won't mention what you might do otherwise," she said.

"Let's have bygones be bygones," he said.

"Easy for you to say."

"I'm more concerned about the future than the past," he said.

"What future?" she said incredulously.

"The future of our child."

"It's not going to have a future. I've got an appointment to end it in eleven more days." Darlene lifted her chin towards him in defiance.

"That's what I want to talk to you about."

"Oh, come on." Darlene swung her arms onto her hips. "Don't get all preachy and righteous on me."

"I'm not getting preachy on you. I'm getting personal."

"What are you talking about?" Darlene said sharply, her voice rising in pitch.

"I'm talking about how I always, *always* wanted a child, and none of my wives ever got pregnant. Not for lack of trying. I never had a chance to have a child. A son or a daughter, it doesn't matter, and here you are pregnant with my child. You said so yourself! For me, it's the chance of a lifetime! Don't you see?"

"See what?" said Darlene in a cracked voice. "Are you delusional? Are you seriously asking me to have this child for you?"

"Yes! Please!" His sky-blue eyes looked pleadingly into her narrowed, suspicious eyes.

Darlene broke her gaze away from his to look down at the carpet. Dazedly, she noticed that it was an orange flower pattern over brown, in an endless repetition. What was she doing looking at the carpet? He had just asked her an outrageous question, and she couldn't think straight. She closed her eyelids to steady herself.

"So, Darlene? What do you think? Will you have my child?" he repeated, coming around the desk to stand next to her.

Darlene vomited on his shoes.

After a stunned silence, Mickey laughed ruefully and said, "I hope that isn't your answer."

Darlene kept her eyes closed in embarrassment. "Can I have a tissue to wipe my mouth and face?"

Mickey reached over to his desk for a handful of tissues and gave them to her. He took a second handful and bent over to wipe his shoes and the carpet. "How long have you had this morning sickness?"

"Since the beginning."

"I was serious, you know," he said quietly, taking her elbow gingerly. "I could pay you a monthly stipend. I guess it would be child support, actually."

Darlene cast her eyes up sideways at him. "Damn right it would be. If I was ever crazy enough to do such a thing."

Mickey's face darkened slightly. "Why do you say it's a crazy thing?"

"To have the child of the man who raped me?"

There was a tense silence between them. It stretched into a painfully long moment as they realized they were trapped in their mutual history.

He said softly, "If I could do it over, I would court you; I would seduce you properly. Little did I know that you would turn out to be the mother of my only child."

Darlene wiped her mouth again with the tissues. Her mouth tasted terrible.

"You are a beautiful woman, Darlene," he began in his smooth, violin voice. "Do you want to go through life never having had a child? Don't you think you should take this opportunity? How many more chances in your life will you have to bear a child?"

He has a point, thought Darlene. I do want a child, someday. But his child? This child?

"How old are you, Darlene?"

She smiled bitterly. "Thirty-five."

"So how many more chances have you got?"

"A few," she said defiantly. But not many, she knew. She didn't have the money for fancy medical fertilization techniques. Just the natural chances her own body would give her. She sighed heavily.

"Think about it, Darlene. I'm willing to sign papers acknowledging paternity now, if you want me to, before the baby is even born, so you can be guaranteed child support." He looked at her.

Her face was impassive.

"Think about how the child support would make life easier for you. You wouldn't have to work so hard. Wouldn't you like to slow down and enjoy life a little?"

Yes, I would, she thought to herself. She said nothing aloud.

"Think about how your grandmother would be so happy if she saw you with your child. Her great-grandchild."

"How do you know about my grandmother?"

"I know your parents were killed in a car crash years ago, and you were an only child raised by your grandmother. Don't you think you should have a child to carry on the family line?"

"How do you know this about me?"

"I have ears."

"Probably spies in all the wrong places."

Mickey grinned. "Whatever. Whaddya say we draw up the papers?"

"Isn't that a bit hasty?"

"Not if it'll keep you from ending the pregnancy."

"That again."

"Yes. That again. That's why everything's so urgent."

Darlene closed her eyes. Away from the intensity of his oh-so-blue eyes and the sound of his violin voice she would be able to think a little more clearly. She would have to think it over carefully.

It was true: she did want a baby. And Mickey Quinn was handsome, intelligent, and daring. Not bad attributes for a child. If she took him up on his offer of child support, it would certainly make life easier. But then her life would be forever bound together with his. Did she want that?

She turned to face him. "The only thing I can tell you now is that I'll think about it. I can't promise anything more."

CHAPTER 21

Tonight would make or break the rebellion against the political establishment. The recall petitions they had filed had proven to have had more than enough signatures to be valid. Now they had to choose candidates to run against the three selectmen in that recall election. Would anybody step up to the challenge?

Maureen was nervous. It showed in the way she bustled around the kitchen, filling the sugar jar to the brim, then overfilling it, spilling grains onto the wooden table which she had to wipe up.

Robert was nervous, too, but he manifested it by sitting absolutely still, listening to the grasshoppers sing on the lawn outside amid the voices of his children playing tag. He kept his eyes trained on the square of window over the sink where he could concentrate on the setting sun with its spectacular display of pinks, oranges, and purples, waiting for people to arrive.

Soon they heard the sound of cars pulling into their long, curved driveway, and they smiled at one another, relieved. In a matter of minutes the kitchen was filled with people, and Maureen found herself busily pouring coffee and tea. "Come, everyone," she said. "Let's move to the front room where all the chairs are set up."

People arranged themselves in a circle in the parlor and began talking to one another animatedly. Most of them held sheaves of petitions in their hands.

"Okay, people!" said Robert, loudly. The chatter

stopped suddenly. "If it's alright with everybody, I'd like to get down to business. Attorney Ebert is here to explain what else we need to do."

Anna stood up, a slight, impeccably-groomed figure in a room filled with a circle of attentive faces. "You all realize that we have to pick the candidates to run against the selectmen we're trying to recall. It's no good getting someone out of office unless you have someone else to replace him with." She watched as the realization began to sink into their minds. "That means that some of you have to be willing to run for office."

She watched their gazes turn inward as they contemplated that thought.

"I say Robert Jaston should run against that slick Gerald Hopper," said a man seated in back.

"I was afraid someone would say that," said Robert. "But I can't run. This whole thing is about me and my farm. It would seem too nakedly self-interested."

"That's exactly why you should run," said Anna. "Who better represents the average person who falls prey to eminent domain than you?"

Robert sighed deeply. "I suppose if I don't step forward, I can't ask any of you to do so, either." He smiled wryly. "I'm running, I guess. But I'll need help with the campaign, big-time. I'm certainly no politician."

"You have us," said Mr. Rutherford. "We'll get you through it."

"That's one selectman down. But there's two more. Anyone else willing to run against them?" asked Anna.

Mr. Rutherford harrumphed, then said, "I will. I'm

an old-timer. There's not too much they can do to me."

"Don't be so sure about that," said a woman to his left. "They'll find something to do, like hike your taxes extra high, or turn off the street light in front of your house."

"If they try that, I'll give 'em hell," he replied.

"Who do you want to run against?" asked Anna Ebert.

"That weasel Danny Tripiano."

"You got it," said Anna Ebert. "Now is there anyone willing to run against Marilyn Hardy?"

A silence descended over the room. Finally, a tiny voice from the corner was heard.

"I will."

"What brave person said that?" asked Robert.

"Me," said Diane Meehan. She was a buxom blonde with twinkling blue eyes and an unexpectedly tiny voice.

"Are you sure you want to take this on?" asked Robert. "Politics can be brutal."

"I know that. But it's important, and it'll be quite the experience."

"You're not kidding. And you've got Marilyn Hardy to thank for that."

"I'm sure I won't be thanking her," said Diane.

"Alright, then. We've got our slate of candidates. Everyone needs to go to town hall, the town clerk's office, as soon as possible and get candidate's petitions. They need to be signed by one hundred registered voters, each," explained Anna. "We'll be meeting again to get the campaigns going in the coming weeks and as the recall election goes forward. Thank you, everyone, and good night."

CHAPTER 22

First came the battle of the lawn signs. That was a quick education as to who their real friends and supporters were. Maureen had telephoned everyone that she and Robert knew in town to ask them if they would put up a lawn sign that said *Robert Jaston, Selectman*. Many were sympathetic but lacked the courage to openly declare against the town leadership.

Robert and his son, Jacob, drove slowly through Longbottom, stopping at each of the houses that had agreed to post a sign for him. It was tiresome, getting in and out of the truck, over and over again. Jacob bent over to hold the sign straight while Robert kneeled to pound the wooden stake into the lawn. Robert's left knee of his jeans was sodden from the wet of the lawns that had soaked up the recent rains.

They pounded in yet another sign in front of a large Cape Cod-style house set back from the road. Finished, they hoisted themselves into the truck and drove to the next house, which was eight houses further up the street. A white sedan came roaring up behind them and stopped behind the truck, inches away from the rear fender. A woman of about age thirty-five got out of the car, carrying their sign. She slammed her car door and rushed towards them. "How dare you put your sign on my lawn!" said the woman, her tawny hair blowing about her face in the wind.

Robert answered mildly, "So sorry, Mrs. Kilroy.

We've gotten permission for every sign location. I see from my list here that we got permission from your husband, a Mr. Kevin Kilroy. Didn't he tell you about it?"

"Nooooo," said Mrs. Kilroy.

"Is it okay with you then?"

"I guess so."

"So we'll go put the sign back up. I hope both of you'll vote for me, too!"

He smiled broadly, to show no hard feelings.

Mrs. Kilroy smiled back at him lopsidedly. She turned, got in her car, and drove away in a flurry, leaving the sign abandoned at the side of the road.

Robert bent over to pick it up and brushed some mud off one side. He slung it in the back of the truck. He and Jacob got back in the pickup and reversed direction.

It was an aggravation, retracing their steps. "You'd think that husband and wife would talk to each other, you know?" said Robert to his son.

Jacob just wiped the sweat off his upper lip.

***

Gerald Hopper was secretly outraged that he had to run against a farmer. In his opinion, being a farmer ought to disqualify someone from running for office. Everyone knew that farmers were rubes, hicks, and bumpkins. They didn't have a forward-thinking idea in their heads. They were all reactionary. Just look at this Jaston fellow. Instead of even negotiating to sell his land, he refused to discuss it. The stubborn bastard had

117

forced them into using eminent domain. Now he had the audacity to organize a recall election. This stubborn bastard wouldn't stop. The only thing to do was to beat him. Beat him in the recall election, and beat him down good.

Beat him into a pulp if need be.

Gerald took care in his election materials to point out that Robert Jaston had never shown any interest before in public service. Only when his land was involved did Robert Jaston show any interest in town politics. That was the ultimate example of a special interest. And everyone knew that special interests were the bane of decent, honorable politics.

Worse still, Robert Jaston was not even an honorable man. Gerald Hopper started a rumor that Robert watered down his milk, which was why he could only sell his milk to jails and prisons. When people asked wasn't it true that Robert Jaston sold his milk to the dairy cooperative, instead, Gerald Hopper shook his head mysteriously, and muttered phrases about rescinded licenses.

As long as he was muttering vague, inflammatory phrases, Gerald decided he might as well throw around a few that would help his fellow selectmen. He started the rumor that Diane Meehan was a lesbian. Since she wasn't married, he figured that rumor would have some legs to it. Marilyn Hardy would be pleased with that one.

Gerald thought about what he could tag onto Mr. Rutherford that would stick. Secret drinker? Secret gambler? Womanizer? Pervert that liked little boys? No-

- no one would believe that of him. Near bankruptcy? Dishonest in business dealings?

Maybe he would leave Mr. Rutherford alone and just get even with him later, somehow.

***

"I can't take much more of people staring at me when I go into town," said Maureen one evening at dinner. She placed her fork down on her plate, even though it was still half full.

"How do you think I feel?" said Jacob, lifting his black eyes up to her. "The kids at school are all in my face about Dad running for selectman."

"In what way?" asked Maureen.

"There was almost a fight. Except that the football coach walked by just then, so everybody walked away."

"Who was going to fight?" asked Robert. "You?"

Jacob looked down at his hands. "I was gonna try to get out of it. I don't want to fight."

"Don't fight, Jacob. This is not about physical fights. We take our fights to the ballot box. The ballot box is the civilized way to fight in a democracy. You tell them that," said Robert, chin raised, eyes trained on Jacob.

"Okay, Dad. Civics lesson over for tonight. I get it."

"Good." Robert's equally black eyes twinkled. "Anyway, how do you think I feel? I'm the one crazy enough to be the candidate!"

"Imagine how you'll feel if you get elected!" said Maureen with a choked laugh.

Robert twisted his mouth into a wry smile. "I'll be hip-deep in it then!"

"Deeper, darling. Much, much deeper. But I'll throw you a life-preserver."

CHAPTER 23

"Who the hell is this Sophie Parsons?" said Mickey Quinn in a low, penetrating voice. He was sitting at his usual back-corner booth in his establishment. Surrounding him were friends and toadies. It was sometimes hard to distinguish who was what because when Mickey got angry he treated everyone with equal contempt.

"She lives over in the next town, I hear," said Denton Clay, who had been summoned once more, for no reason that he could discern.

"Who does she think she is, drawing these political cartoons? She's making us look like asses."

No one at the table spoke, which was confirmation enough.

"Can we sue the bitch? Or this rag of a newspaper which is printing these obscenities?" asked Mickey, turning to Tobias.

"I'm afraid not," Tobias grumbled as he made a face of disgust. "You see, libel law says that the truth is an absolute defense. I checked out the quotes attributed to each of the selectmen, and they're taken from actual public meetings. There are public video-recordings of these meetings, and those public records would be proof of the quotes used."

"But the quotes make the selectmen sound so stupid and vile," complained Mickey.

"They have only themselves to blame for any

stupidities that come out of their mouths," responded Tobias.

"But these cartoons will turn public opinion against us in the long run," said Mickey. "We ought to be trying to win this thing."

"We will," said Tobias. "Anyway, we have Rufus to count on if things get sticky."

Denton went very still, wondering if he was supposed to have heard that. He didn't consider himself a confidante of Mickey Quinn, and he figured the less he knew, the better. On the other hand, Mickey had an undue hold on him: maybe it would be an advantage to know a few uncomfortable truths about Mickey.

Denton studiously kept his eyes on the table, not meeting anyone's gaze, trying to keep everyone's attention off of him. He was small, and if he was motionless, he could even fade into the woodwork. He would not say anything more for the remainder of the afternoon.

"Find out what you can about this Sophie Parsons," said Mickey, "and start some nasty rumors about her." He directed this comment to the table in general. Each of them was supposed to make it their personal mission to carry out his latest directive.

There was general nodding and grunts of assent, but no one grabbed it as their own.

"By next week I want to hear some dirt on her. Got it?"

The nods were bigger and fiercer this time.

CHAPTER 24

The Saturday morning of the recall election arrived on a brisk, windy, November day. Robert Jaston was stirring at four a.m. and milking his cows by five in the darkness before the cool, thin dawn. When the milking was done, he returned to the farmhouse to shower and get dressed for the ordeal ahead of him. The polls opened at seven, and he wanted to be there to greet the very first voters.

The scent of cinnamon in simmering oatmeal met his nose as he shaved in the upstairs bathroom. He was extra careful to not bloody himself with a careless stroke. He certainly didn't want to show up to the polls with a snippet of tissue clinging to his face. Sighing, he combed down his thick, black hair which was still wet from the shower. Finally, he donned his one and only suit, matching tie, and dress shoes. He was as ready as he would ever be. He gave himself a final glance in the bureau mirror, made a face, and turned to go downstairs to the kitchen.

Maureen stood at the stove, stirring the pot of oatmeal. Clear, gray light slanted through the kitchen window onto the metal sink next to the stove. "Good morning, sweetheart! Ready for today?" she asked. She stood in her robe and slippers, her hair slightly mussed from sleep. Robert stood next to her and twisted to kiss her on the mouth.

"Hardly," he said. "This election is like birthing a calf. You wait and wait, and then when it finally comes, it's a bloody mess."

"But think of the valuable calf. The result will save our farm," she reminded him.

"We'll see." He looked grim.

Maureen dished out two bowls of oatmeal. She and Robert sat down in silence and ate. Their three children were sleeping later on a Saturday morning, and wouldn't be down for another hour. Jacob was assigned the job of babysitting the twins since both Robert and Maureen expected to be at the polls all day.

"I'll go upstairs and get ready," Maureen said softly when they were done eating. "I'll have the twins do the dishes for us later today."

She rose and carried the bowls and spoons to the metal sink and stacked them. "Help yourself to coffee, Robert. It's on the stove. We can fill a thermos with coffee to go. Oh, and I made sandwiches for the kids, and for us to take."

Robert smiled slightly for the first time. "You're alright, baby."

"Thanks."

Fifteen minutes later they drove into Longbottom's high school parking lot. The high school was a squat, single-story, brick building. The parking lot itself was unevenly patched, and a few early-bird voters' cars were already parked randomly. Robert parked their truck as close to the front entrance as he was allowed to and shut off the engine. He stepped out, reached into the bed of his truck, and pulled up a tri-cornered wooden sign that had his campaign posters on all three sides. He stood it up in the bed of his truck.

"This here is our campaign headquarters for the day," he announced to Maureen.

"Okay," she said.

Robert looked around to see who was already there. He saw the three selectmen standing in a line in front of the school entrance. They were lined up to shake hands with the voters, one at a time. He ought to be over there, too. There was a brisk wind that blew in uneven bursts, and swirled around the corners of the building. It brought a bright flush to noses and cheek and left people glassy-eyed. Robert was aware of his own nose starting to run in the cold, and he self-consciously wiped his sleeve across his face.

Anna Ebert approached him from behind, startling him. "How's it going?"

"Okay, I guess. I should be in that gauntlet over there."

"You should," she chided him gently.

"I'm going, I'm going."

"Good. I can keep you company over there. Or Maureen can. Whomever you want," said Anna.

"Maybe you for a while, to make sure things are legit."

As Robert and Anna neared the school entrance, Diane Meehan and Mr. Rutherford arrived.

Diane was visibly upset. "Did you notice Marilyn Hardy's big sign at the end of the school parking lot driveway by the street?"

"No," said Anna. "What about it?"

"Her huge sign is conspicuously splattered with bright red paint! Made to look as if I did it! As if I ever did such a thing!" said Diane Meehan. She made a pfftting sound as her lips rattled in disgust. "I bet she did it herself to gain sympathy."

"Do you think she'd be that devious?" asked Robert.

"I have no doubt she's capable of something that devious," said Anna.

"The problem is proving it."

"And the damage is already done," said Diane bitterly.

They fell silent as they contemplated just what they were up against.

"We have to go forward, regardless," said Robert. "Are our poll-watchers here yet?"

"All in place," said Anna. "Sophie had no trouble getting people for you."

"Great," said Mr. Rutherford. "Let's get going. Time to greet the voters."

The day passed in a dizzying sweep of voters going past them one by one, or in groups of two or three. Robert's right hand began to become sore from shaking so many hands. He shivered from the bursts of cold wind that rushed over his face and neck. He wished he could go inside. Unfortunately, greeting voters was not allowed inside the building. Being a candidate was an endurance test.

Inside, the poll-watchers for Robert Jaston and his fellow candidates were keeping track of who came in to vote during the day. Those who had pledged support of the Jaston/Meehan/Rutherford team who had not made it to the polls near the end of the day, would be called to come to vote before the polls closed.

Anna meandered about the gymnasium. She wandered closer to a table of election-day workers who were busy with a stack of punch card ballots. The election-day workers were all people appointed by Rufus Fishbane to work the election.

She wondered why the punch card ballots were not in the hands of actual voters. She inched over closer to see what they were doing. To her amazement, the election-day workers were punching particular holes on the ballots. Anna Ebert stood directly over the table but the election-day workers never looked up from continuing to mark the ballots. The completed ballots were stacked in a pile against the wall.

"What are you doing?" asked Anna.

"Oh, we're just practicing with some of the ballots," answered one election-day worker airily. She fingered the ballot with a brightly painted nail and smiled from her seat at the table.

"Practicing for election fraud, are we?" asked Anna.

The election-day worker gave her a nasty look, her smile gone.

"I'm the attorney for three of the candidates here today. Jaston, Meehan, and Rutherford. I say you'd better tear up those ballots immediately, or I'll report each of you to the election commission. What are your names?" Anna reached into her voluminous handbag and took out a small notepad and a pen. She was poised to write.

"Oh, alright," grumbled one of the other election-day workers. She reached across the other worker to the pile and took a handful. Slowly and methodically, she began ripping the punch card ballots into small pieces. The worker with the painted nails sat motionless and watched her.

"I just wanted to make sure that your 'practice' ballots didn't end up intermingled with the rest of the ballots," said Anna.

The woman with the painted nails rolled her eyes at the suggestion.

"I'll be stopping by frequently today, to make sure you ladies don't start up any more 'practice' ballots, understand?"

Across the gymnasium, Rufus was loudly talking and laughing with a group of townies who stood in an aggressively large circle. As they raucously laughed, they surveyed the room for who had come by to vote. The ordinary townspeople who voted studiously avoided eye contact with the townies. All afternoon, they silently came and went, giving no indication of their political stance.

Just after dinnertime, Maureen drove back to the farm to pick up Jacob, Layla, and Shaina. She wanted the entire family to be together when the results were announced. Maureen went inside to vote. Their three children stood outside with their father in the darkness of the November night. The polls were due to close at eight.

Rufus emerged from the front doors of the high school. "Twenty more minutes, folks, and it'll be all over." He grinned wickedly and ducked back into the warmth of the high school.

Robert waited until his watch said eight to go inside with his children. The yellow lights in the cavernous gymnasium cast harsh shadows on people's faces.

People looked as tired as he felt. Yet underneath his fatigue, he felt adrenaline begin to take hold. He reached out both hands to take the hands of his ten-year-old twin daughters. His son, Jacob, stood to one side, expressionless, waiting for something to happen.

"Come! The machines are tallying the votes in the office across the hall," said Anna.

Just then, Maureen joined the family cluster.

Robert and his family followed everyone down the hallway to the office where the tabulator machine was clicking away. Several election-day workers sauntered about the room, watching the machine idly. Maureen looked at Robert and saw that he was staring at the machine intently, as if he was trying to will it to the correct outcome.

Suddenly the machine stopped. A narrow paper receipt issued from the top. An election-day worker reached for it, and read it. She was entirely expressionless. Then she handed it to Rufus Fishbane, who placed it on his clipboard, where it was no longer visible.

Rufus cleared his throat, to signal that he was about to read the election results. "Gerald Hopper: 2013 votes. Robert Jaston: 1194 votes."

Robert felt a stone settle in the bottom of his belly. He clutched his daughters' hands fiercely. "Daddy!" they whispered. "You're hurting!"

What were the other results? If only he could keep a

clear head to listen.

"Daniel Tripiano: 1987 votes. John Rutherford: 806 votes." Damn.

"Marilyn Hardy: 2001 votes. Diane Meehan: 794 votes." Shit.

Rufus Fishbane began shaking the hands of the winners. There was a ragged, belated cheer from several of the townies who had crowded in to hear the results.

Suddenly, Robert heard Anna Ebert talking. She was requesting to see the actual tally slip that came from the machine. She was on the heels of Rufus Fishbane, who was doing his very best to ignore her. Rufus put his sheaf of papers and his clipboard under his arm and serenely marched out of the office and into the lobby of the high school. There he put on his leather jacket and scarf and marched out of the building to his car.

Anna furiously followed him out into the parking lot.

"Let's go home, honey," said Maureen tiredly.

"While we still have a home, that is," said Robert.

The five of them climbed silently into their truck. Robert drove home in the dark, wondering how many more times he would make this drive.

As they approached the farm, Robert felt warm tears pool inside his eyelids, but he blinked them away. Maureen, riding shotgun, couldn't see them, which was just as well.

Once home, the children sensed their parents wanted to be alone, and skedaddled upstairs.

"I wonder how long we've got," said Maureen quietly, over a cup of tea.

"We've just got as long as that notice gives us. Half that time is gone."

"Oh, Robert, our lives are ruined."

"Remember what I said at the beginning?"

"What?"

"Over my dead body will they take this farm!"

Maureen studied him. "Don't do anything crazy, sweetheart."

Robert began to laugh a staccato laugh. "No way, baby."

CHAPTER 25

Mickey Quinn, seated at his usual corner table in his pub, lifted his beer mug high, spilling a bit of foam, as the three selectmen entered. He watched as they made their way slowly across the room through a throng of well-wishers. A little smile played on the corners of his mouth. He turned to Tobias Meachum, "Not a bad day, huh?"

"Sweet as a seventeen-year-old sex kitten."

Gerald Hopper, Danny Tripiano, and Marilyn Hardy now stood before them, waiting to be invited to join them.

Mickey stretched out the moment. "So, to the newly re-elected selectmen and selectwoman, congratulations!"

"Thanks."

"Sit down, won'tcha?"

The three hastily took their seats in loose chairs.

"We couldn't have done it without you, Mr. Quinn," said Danny Tripiano, leaning elbows-in onto the table. "We owe you."

"Big-time," confirmed Mickey. He took a leisurely swig from his beer mug, wiped the foam off his upper lip, and regarded them through lids at half-mast.

"You really turned out the vote, Mr. Quinn," said Marilyn Hardy, with an appreciative nod and an impish smile. "I'm ready to celebrate! How about a drink?"

Mickey gestured to the waitress to come over. "This round is on the house."

"A margarita for me," said Marilyn. "I can't forget those I had at your house, that your lovely wife made."

"Yeah, that Clarisse is something, alright." He smiled slightly. "And you two?"

"A draft beer for me," said Gerald. He gestured towards Mickey's mug. "Whatever you're having."

"The house Merlot," said Danny, scratching a hairy ear as he winked up at the waitress. She clicked her lips, wrote their orders, and walked away.

"Toby, maybe you oughta tell 'em."

"Tell us what?" asked Gerald in a hushed voice.

"Listen carefully, kiddies," said Mickey, with a wicked grin on his face. "Gather 'round, as they say." He leaned in towards the center of the table.

The others hunched into the center until their heads were almost touching.

The waitress arrived with their drinks and they sprang back. They reached for their drinks and took deep swallows of alcohol, as if to steel themselves against whatever was coming.

"As you were about to say, Toby?" Mickey's eyes glittered.

Tobias turned his angular face towards the three selectmen and broke into a slowly-opening grin. "We didn't exactly turn out the vote," he said. "Rather, we *turned* the vote."

"I don't understand," said Gerald, wondering if he was hearing correctly against the roar of background noise in the pub.

"We turned in the vote we needed."

"How did you manage that?"

133

"By giving the higher vote count of each race to you."

"What do you mean?"

"If the farmer won by 503 votes, we announced that it was you who had won by 503 votes. We reversed the totals," said Tobias.

"Holy shit!" exclaimed Gerald. "How do we expect to get away with that?"

"Don't worry, the vote tally receipts have already been put under lock and key. No one will see them," said Mickey.

"How can you be so sure?" asked Gerald uneasily.

"Relax, my man. All is taken care of. Now cheer up, take that stupid scowl off your ugly mug, or someone will definitely suspect you."

Gerald put on a fake smile and reached for his stein of beer.

"You two stooges. Look alive. This is supposed to be a celebration. Jesus, Mary, and Joseph, you three are lame."

The waitress returned, asking them if they wanted another round. She bent over, displaying her cleavage to Mickey, who laughed and slapped the table.

As the three ordered another round of drinks, Marilyn frowned disapprovingly at the waitress. Danny rolled his eyes at Marilyn and smiled ingratiatingly at the waitress, who ignored him and walked away.

"So why are you three all so glum about this election?" asked Mickey. "Are you upset that you lost to that farmer and his friends? What do you care? You've been declared the winners!"

"I like to think I was elected in my own right," said Gerald.

"Well, get over it," said Tobias. "You weren't."

"So what happens now?" asked Danny.

"We wait and see," said Tobias.

"For what?"

"To see if that farmer and his friends are smart enough to ask for a recount. That could complicate things," said Tobias, pursing his lips.

"Why?" asked Danny.

Tobias looked at him as if he was an imbecile. "Obviously, running the ballots through the ballot machine again will yield the real results. Which are not favorable to you and your team. Do I make myself clear?"

Danny was silent. He swallowed hard.

"We better hope and pray he doesn't ask for a recount," said Marilyn. She looked down at her hands, which were clasped tightly in prayer-fashion. "Hell's bells. I may even have to go back to church to pray."

"Let's not be over-dramatic, Marilyn. It'll all work out," said Mickey.

"So I guess I'll be seeing you three around, then, huh?" dismissing them from the discussion and the table.

Chapter 26

Michael Quinn had thought about only one thing for the past week. And it wasn't the re-election of the selectmen, even though that had turned out very satisfactorily. So far.

No. The thing that kept him up at night, next to his sleeping wife, Clarisse, was the thought that another woman, Darlene, was pregnant with his only child. If only he could persuade her to go through with the pregnancy.

The post-election crowd had finally left his establishment, and he and Darlene were alone in the place. He knew he had to attract her attention before she left for the night. He intended to find out her plans. He sidled up to the door of his office and peeked around it to see what she was doing.

Darlene stretched upwards to reach the overhead wineglass rack. She slid the still-steaming-hot wineglasses into their slots above the bar. The dishwasher was open a crack and billowed steam upwards towards the mirror behind the bar. Next, she bent to empty the coolers of their melted ice.

"Darlene," he called out gently as he approached her at the bar.

"What?"

He smiled. A charming smile, she thought.

"You look especially pretty tonight, with your hair all disheveled."

She looked down and continued wiping the bar with the cloth rag.

"You know that we have some unfinished business, you and I."

"I know what you're going to say."

"Well, let me say it again. Indulge me."

Darlene looked at him sidelong, still wiping the counter.

"You know that I'm desperate to have a child. My third wife and I have been unable to conceive. None of my wives have ever had my kid. You're my last hope."

"I know."

"And you know that I'm willing to support you handsomely if you bear this child."

Darlene nodded.

"Will you please, please, do this? Even though it began all wrong?"

Darlene nodded again, looking glum.

"You will?"

"Yes."

"Really?" He grinned broadly. "Why didja change your mind?"

Darlene gave him a stern look. "Believe me, it had nothing to do with you. Or what you want." She hesitated. "I had a dream..." Darlene began, then flushed, as she realized that sounded foolish. "Well, first I had a dream about the baby. I dreamed it was a blonde, laughing, baby, but I couldn't see its face, and I couldn't tell if it was a boy or girl. But I didn't think much about the dream by itself.

"But then I went to visit my grandmother. She

looked at me, and immediately said, 'You're with child!' She saw that in me, even though I hadn't told her yet. I asked her how she knew, and she said, 'I can see it in your eyes, your smile, and in the way you carry yourself.' She said that my being pregnant made her very happy, even though I wasn't yet married. She was happy that there was going to be another member in a long line of family. She predicted a girl."

"This is great!" said Mickey, opening his arms wide to embrace her.

Darlene pointedly avoided his embrace. He pretended not to notice. "How do you think your grandmother knew?"

"My grandmother has the 'gift' of seeing the unseen. She's part Indian, Cree, a tribe from up Montana and Canada way. She can see the unborn within me. She can see the hidden parts of a person, and whether they are a good or evil person. She wants to meet you, to take your measure."

"I'll meet her. I'm not afraid," he said.

Darlene smirked.

"I'm not. I've got nothing to hide."

"Just the fact that you already have a wife, and that you're a rapist."

"So what to all that," he said in a calm tone of voice. "She'll see I'm ready to love the child. That's what matters."

"Yes. The child. If I'm going to do this, you need to sign those papers, now. By tomorrow or the next day at the latest."

"Of course."

"I'm not foolin', Mickey."

"I know."

"If you don't come up with those papers fast, I'll sue you for paternity once the child's born, and make a big public scandal, right here in Longbottom. Embarrass your lovely wife."

"Okay, okay. I'll get my lawyer-buddy, Toby, on it right away."

"Okay, then. Just so we understand each other. And don't think I'm doing this for you or anything. Don't get any stuck-up ideas like that. I'm doing this for my grandmother and me."

"But I'll have visitation rights with the child."

"Yeah. Some. But she'll be raised by me. Period."

Mickey scratched his blond hair bemusedly. We'll see about all that, he thought. But one step at a time. But then again, would Clarisse accept another woman's child?

Problems seem to crop up wherever he turned. Whatever. He had won today.

Tomorrow would take care of itself.

CHAPTER 27

The Longbottom town hall was locked and dark at two a.m. There were no cars in the vicinity until a small sedan approached with its lights off, and came to a stop half a block away. The engine shut off, and a figure got out of the car. It was hard to make out the gender of the person under the sliver of moonlight. The black night shadows of the trees obscured that person's approach. The slim figure tiptoed across the pavement to the side entrance of town hall and entered stealthily. The individual's hand reached into a coat pocket and pulled out a key. The side door was unlocked and the intruder eased inside. Through a window, there was a vague impression of a flashlight being momentarily turned on. The key code was quickly punched in to dismantle the alarm.

The person walked down the hallway to Rufus Fishbane's office. Through a different window this time, there was the faintest hint of yellow light around the edges of the pulled shades. The flashlight shone on Rufus's desk. The intruder began to look through the papers on top of his desk, then inside the drawers. In the upper right drawer was the bonanza: the voting machine tabulations on strips of paper. That person took the papers over to the copier machine in the corner of the office and turned on the copier. It made a whirring noise. It took two long minutes for the copier to warm up. When it was ready, that person made multiple copies of the voting tabulations. The individual looked around the office for something to verify the copies. The intruder smiled while reaching for the date stamp labeled "Town Clerk, Town of Longbottom". That person stamped each copy with the town clerk's date stamper, then folded them up, and put them away in a coat pocket. The original tabulation papers were returned to their place in Rufus Fishbane's desk. The person then remembered to turn off the copier machine and pick up the flashlight.

The intruder left quietly, turned the alarm back on, locked the door, and drove away with no lights on the car. The individual returned home without the family hearing anything, and breathed a sigh of relief. The copies of the voting tabulations were hidden in a special place, deep in the lower kitchen cabinets, amidst the pots and pans rarely used. The person went to bed, trembling with exhilaration at what had just been accomplished.

CHAPTER 28

Words of accusation formed on Clarisse's tongue. Her mouth felt molten, loose, and dangerous. She pinched her lips together to seal them against her tongue. Words of anger rose every time her good-for-nothing husband, Michael Quinn, reached across the bed for her.

Clarisse knew he had been with another woman, but he gave no overt indication. Yet whenever she looked him directly in the eyes, his pupils got smaller in his oh-so-blue eyes. As if he were withdrawing from her questions before they could be asked.

"Mickey," whispered Clarisse.

"What?"

"Don't you think we should go to a clinic for that fertility testing, like we talked about before?"

Mickey jerked away from her, involuntarily. "Why are you suddenly on that old subject again?"

"I thought you wanted a child more than anything."

"I do."

"Well then?"

"I thought we'd let nature take its course a little longer."

Clarisse felt her heart drop in her chest. She now knew with absolute clarity that there was another woman, and something had occurred to make Michael Quinn place his hopes in this nameless other woman, rather than Clarisse. She reached a hand out to tentatively stroke his chest hair. "Am I still your sweetie?"

"Of course, babe." He gazed at her through half-lidded eyes.

She caressed him as she layed on her side on the bed. He smiled at her, a touch sadly, it seemed. He caught her hand on his chest, entangled in his golden chest hairs. For an instant she thought he was about to confess. He lay very still, as if considering, and then the moment passed.

But now she knew she was just the side dish. Her Michael Quinn had moved on, somehow, to another woman. It was only a matter of time before he decided to divorce her, like he had the others. But she still had some time. She had to figure out a plan.

***

Clarisse had decided to do a thorough search of Michael's papers, to see what he was up to. She had waited until he had left the house to search his desk in the den.

A painstaking search turned up a few interesting items: an oversized envelope full of snapshots of scantily-clothed women hugging Michael in various suggestive poses; a list of names of prominent citizens of Longbottom with percentages posted next to their names, and no further explanation; old copies of his parents' wills; a manila envelope with the name "Darlene" written on the front in blue ink; and an envelope containing a life insurance policy for $500,000.00 taken out on Clarisse's life.

She hadn't known he had taken out the policy on her. She shivered as she considered the implications. Did he want her dead before he moved on to his next woman? She would have to be mighty careful.

Meanwhile, who were all of these women, scantily clad, wrapped around her husband's torso? She could only hope they were from the days before their marriage.

And who was this Darlene, who merited her own envelope in his desk? The envelope was sealed, but Clarisse decided to steam it open in the kitchen, using her favorite teapot. The teapot was whistling harshly when the telephone rang.

"Hello?" answered Clarisse.

"Hi, Babe. It's me," said Michael Quinn.

"What's up?"

"Just wanted to tell you that maybe we should consider adoption. You know. As an alternative."

"Isn't that kinda coming out of the blue? What about us going to the clinic as a first step, like I suggested?" said Clarisse.

"Well, you know, maybe speed up the process somewhat. Just a thought. Is that the teapot making all that racket?"

"Yeah. I was just about to make a cup when you called."

"Enjoy. I'll see you later tonight."

She hung up the phone shakily. It was as if he had an eerie intuition that she was going to steam open his papers with the teapot when he called.

Clarisse held up the manila envelope to the steam.

The glue released, and the flap opened. She reached inside for the papers. What she saw astonished her. Her husband was acknowledging paternity of a child conceived by a woman named Darlene Bundt. Furthermore, he was agreeing to financially support the child throughout childhood, until age twenty-one. The child had not been born yet but was due sometime in the month of March. This agreement became valid upon the birth of the child.

Clarisse lowered her trembling hands that held the papers. *Oh, the lying bastard.*

She saw through him now. He wanted to arrange to adopt the child that was already his by another woman. And he would pass the child off as adopted to her. And she would have to pretend that she was none the wiser.

A sudden chill went through her. Unless he intended to do her in and to raise his child with this Darlene Bundt character. Maybe he wanted her out of the way. After all, he had purchased the life insurance policy on her.

Clarice pulled the screaming teapot up and put it to rest on a cool burner.

She pulled a tea bag out of the canister, dropped it in the waiting mug, and poured the boiling water over the it. The tea billowed steam. She leaned over the tea cup and inhaled the aroma. She needed to collect her thoughts. If she wasn't careful, the consequences would be very, very bad. She would end up very, very dead.

CHAPTER 29

Deer-hunting season had begun, and Robert Jaston had an excuse to take his rifle out of its locked cabinet in the front room. He methodically began to clean it, polish it, and check his ammunition over several days.

Each time, Maureen watched him out of the corner of her eye from the doorway. She was leery of guns and didn't want them around, but Robert insisted that deer were destructive to farms and needed to be culled every year. Plus, he had a yearly hankering for venison, he claimed.

It was a Friday night. The days had grown short. Robert had dressed in layers to ward off the chill of the season. "I'm going to be out tonight, and into the wee hours of the morning," he said. "Have Jacob do the morning milking. No school on Saturday. And he's old enough now." His face was expressionless.

Maureen felt an alarm go off deep in the back of her mind, but she couldn't muster the necessary words. She felt the floor tilting under her feet. "Okay." She closed her eyes for a long moment before turning away and walking back to the kitchen. Ever since Robert and his cohorts had lost the recall election, they had been living on borrowed time at the farm. She walked through her days, grief-stricken.

Robert left before midnight, after drinking three cups of coffee, and took a tall thermos of coffee and a sandwich with him.

Maureen, lying awake in bed upstairs, heard him go. The truck rumbled softly down the road towards Longbottom center.

Robert drove slowly towards Mickey Quinn's house. He stopped a quarter mile short of reaching it, at a roadside clearing that deer hunters often used. He shut off his engine and sat there, listening to the ticking of the engine as it cooled. Then he reached for his rifle, got out of his truck, and ducked into the woods alongside the road. A three-quarter moon was out on the clear night. He waited until his eyes adjusted. Then he began walking towards Mickey Quinn's house, parallel to the road, within the woods.

The forest floor was open in some places, under stands of pine trees. He heard an owl hoot in the distance. At other patches, trees had begun to shed their leaves, and he was conscious of making noise amid those that had fallen.

A black shape flew near his face, probably a bat. He cradled his rifle in his left arm, muzzle pointed to the ground. Later he came to a patch of dense underbrush, where he had to hold his rifle aloft as he trampled through. He hoped he wasn't straying from the road to his left. He strained to make out his vantage point. As he stood motionless, a car drove slowly past. He saw that he was no more than twenty feet away from the road. He smiled grimly and cautiously continued until he could see the outdoor lights shining on Mickey's house, ahead.

Good. Almost there.

Robert stared at Mickey's house in the moonlight. Even in the darkness, it was impressive, with its many windows and shutters, and the expensive landscaping around the house. He could see the lawn was plush, with its scattering of autumn leaves on it. The lawn swelled towards the stately house like a dark tide, and the house rode the crest like an ocean liner. The house built with ill-begotten money, thought Robert. Never, never, will my farm be sold to finance this house and its people, he vowed to himself.

Robert crouched behind an evergreen bush that was located directly across from the Quinns' driveway. Soon he went to kneeling. He thought about how he had told Maureen he was deer hunting. If he didn't come home with a deer, would she become suspicious? Well, he was being truthful when he said he was going hunting.

A car approached from his right, the direction from Longbottom's center. He squinted to see the glints of moonlight on the car as it approached. It was the silver Cadillac.

Robert trembled as he raised his rifle to his shoulder. He lowered his eye to the sights on the gun.

Could he do this?

The Cadillac swung into the driveway and stopped. The garage door began to rise automatically. When it rose fully, the Cadillac drove smoothly into the left side of the garage. The lights went on inside the garage, and Robert saw the driver's door swing open as Mickey began to get out. But the garage door had begun to descend just as Mickey stood up, and his head, then his torso, were covered.

Frustrated, Robert squeezed the trigger at Mickey's legs. A moment later, he watched Mickey Quinn's

Cadillac release a spurt of flames. As the garage door continued its descent, Robert was denied any more view of the scene. He imagined Mickey Quinn fighting the fire with an extinguisher.

No, he would call the fire department before it burned down his house. The fire department would search for a cause of the fire. Would they find the bullet?

The sound of the shot had echoed loudly amidst the quiet of the woods. Yet the sound of the garage door grinding its descent must have been equally loud on that side of the street. Maybe they wouldn't know what hit the car, but he doubted it. He had to get out of there, fast. He burst forth from the forest to the edge of the road. He began running back to his truck. He grew out of breath and had to walk.

Why had he parked so far away? When he caught his breath, he began to run again, heavily. He thought he heard sirens in the distance.

Robert reached his truck at the roadside clearing. He scrambled into it and started the engine without turning on the lights. He definitely heard sirens in the distance. He had to hurry. He pulled onto the road, then turned on his lights. Best to make as if he were an ordinary driver, out for a drive. At two a.m. Right. And he a farmer who had to be up at five a.m. to milk the cows. That was certainly believable. Best to get on home before anyone saw him or his truck on this road. He forced himself to drive the speed limit, in case a police car was approaching from this direction.

Four minutes later, he made a right turn onto

another road that would take him back to his farm in a roundabout way. The sound of sirens had disappeared in the distance.

He longed to be in his bed, curled up next to Maureen. He would get home and stash his gun in its locked cabinet tonight. Best to make as if it had not been out yet this season. He'd milk the cows this morning, himself, as if he'd not gone out hunting after all. Let Jacob go back to bed. Tell Maureen the night had been a bust for hunting. The deer had been nowhere to be seen under the three-quarter moon, he'd say.

The lights of another car were approaching from the opposite direction. Robert fervently hoped it was not a police car on its way to the scene. The headlights flickered through the black tree trunks along the curve of the road. It was indeed one of Longbottom's finest, Robert saw, as the car passed him on the road. He watched intently in his rear-view mirror to see what the police car would do. It continued down the road, away from him. He almost sobbed with relief. Get ahold of yourself, he admonished himself. You'd better get ahold of yourself in front of Maureen.

He made a left turn onto the road that led to his farm and felt a modicum of relief.

Three minutes later he drove into his curved gravel driveway in front of his farmhouse.

He shut off the truck engine. He reached for his rifle, his thermos, his bagged lunch, and got out of the truck, careful to make no noise closing the truck door. He walked to the farmhouse and unlocked the deadbolt silently. He eased into the kitchen and walked to the front room. There he unloaded the rifle, then locked it up in its cabinet. He pocketed the key. Now, if only Maureen was asleep when he got upstairs.

He would be able to face her better in the morning. He'd have to prepare to face her when she heard the news about the fire at Mickey Quinn's house. But by then, he'd have his story straight.

CHAPTER 30

Fire trucks and an ambulance blared sirens on their way to the Quinn house, through the hollow darkness of the winding, wooded roads. Mickey Quinn furiously battled the flames spurting from the trunk of his car, smothering with an old blanket the tongues that licked forth. He figured the can of lighter fluid he had had in the trunk of his car had been struck by a bullet, and thereby ignited. If he could just keep the fire from reaching the gas tank of his car...He knew he should step away, in case the whole car blew, but he wanted to save his beloved Cadillac, and save his dream house from burning down in flames. If only the damned fire department would get here...he'd been so busy swatting at the flames, had anyone called 911? He hoped Clarisse had woken up at the sound of him coming home, and heard the gunshot. And that she had been sharp enough to call 911. He heard the sirens now...good woman...she had called them...Thank God! He continued swatting at the flames as the fire truck drove up his driveway, and the firefighters jumped down to take over.

They brought their fire hoses close, and a powerful stream of water shot at the rear end of the Cadillac. The firefighters pried open the trunk to get at the source of the flames. Then one firefighter used huge pliers to remove the can of lighter fluid. He flung the offending can onto the driveway where it fizzled and sputtered under the deluge of water.

"What were you doing driving around with lighter fluid in your car?" said the lead firefighter to Mickey. "Not looking to commit arson, I hope."

"Naw, not my style," said Mickey. He thrust his chin out and glared at the firefighter. "I get what I want by hiring the best lawyers money can buy." He smirked at his own words.

The firefighter pointedly did not laugh. He was in his late thirties, the son of a former selectman. "I'll have to make a report of the cause of the fire," he said. "That it was started by lighter fluid in the trunk of a car."

"You idiot! The lighter fluid didn't light itself! I was shot at! A bullet came at me, intended for me, and struck the can of lighter fluid, setting it on fire!"

The firefighter's voice remained even. "How do you know you were shot at?"

"Because that's the only explanation!" Mickey's grimy face shone with excitement and sweat under the bright headlights of the fire truck.

"Okay, let's see if we can find a bullet hole. And I better call the police chief in on this, since you think a gun was involved." Rapid phone calls ensued.

Mickey leaned against the frame of his garage. At least his beautiful house hadn't burnt down. He looked at his hands. They were blackened with soot and grease. He couldn't tell if he had blisters from the fire, he was so jazzed up, even though he was simultaneously exhausted.

The door leading from the garage to the house opened, and Clarisse peeked around it. There she was. Nice of her to show up at this juncture, when it was all over, he thought, grimacing sarcastically to himself.

"Mickey! Are you alright?" asked Clarisse.

"Yeah, I guess so." He said. "Except that someone took a shot at me. Which is what started this whole mess."

Clarisse stepped down from her perch in the doorway and walked between the Cadillac and her Subaru to approach her husband. She was dressed only in her nightgown and robe, with her slippers on her feet, which were getting soaked with all the water on the floor of the garage.

She stretched out her hand to his, in a gesture of sympathy. He took her hand, knowing he would dirty it completely.

"What do you mean: someone took a shot at you?" asked Clarisse.

"Someone shot at me, with a bullet, or bullets, and hit the can of lighter fluid in the trunk of my car."

"What was lighter fluid doing in the trunk of your car?"

"Never mind. That's irrelevant. What matters is that someone shot at me!" He flung her hand away from his side.

"Easy, Mickey. Tell it to the cops, and I'm sure they'll figure it out."

"Yeah, they got about the same chance as Elmer Fudd."

"Who's Elmer Fudd?" asked Clarisse.

"Geez, I'm married to someone so young so she doesn't know who Elmer Fudd is?" he said to the night air. Turning to her, he said, "What good are you if you don't even get my jokes?"

"What are you saying? I'm not good enough for you? Are you looking to get rid of me or something?" asked Clarisse, suddenly tearful.

"What? What are you talking about?" Mickey looked at her sharply.

Now I've done it, thought Clarisse. I've given myself away. He'll know I've looked in his desk. "No, sweetie," she said, mustering a winsome smile. "I guess I just get crazy sometimes, the thought of you with all those women at your bar every day, showing up in their skimpy outfits"

"Clarisse, what the hell are you talking about? Our cars and our house nearly burned to a crisp!" He swiveled as a tall, thin figure approached them from the darkness beyond.

"Mr. Quinn, it's Chief Tom Burrill here. I've got a couple of questions. My men have indeed found a bullet hole in your car. Who do you think would've been taking a shot at you?"

Mickey smiled grimly. "I've got some unhappy business rivals."

"Anyone in particular?"

"I'll have to think on it. I'll get back to you."

"Don't take too long." Chief Burrill half-turned away, then turned back. "Just what were you doing with lighter fluid in your trunk?" His lean face, lit faintly by the three-quarter moon, was intensely focused on Mickey Quinn's response. He waited.

Mickey flapped his arms. "I don't remember, exactly. I think it was a leftover item from the summer.

155

You know, from grilling at barbecue time, something like that."

Chief Burrill gave a slight nod and, without further comment, went to his car. He started his engine, turned on his lights, and slowly pulled away in the darkness, half watching the moon as it rode the treetops.

Clarisse turned to Mickey and said, "So who do you think it was that's after you, sweetie?"

"Shut up, babe. I need to think. Just shut the hell up."

Clarisse felt a stirring of rage under her skin at those words. Ungrateful bastard. Treating her like dirt, while he got another woman pregnant.

She felt the rage quietly electrify her limbs, until she felt the very blood flowing under her skin had heated up somehow and was stirring her to action.

What action, she didn't yet know. Time would tell. The rage was seething, not boiling. It wouldn't explode at him just now, but it would slowly find its way to the surface at the right time and place. She was sure of it. And he would be very, very sorry.

CHAPTER 31

Robert Jaston woke to his alarm at 4:30 a.m. He raised his head from the pillow then let it fall back. He slowly stirred his legs and arms under the comforter, feeling like sludge. He had vowed to himself that he would milk the cows this morning and let Jacob go off duty. Best to pretend that last night had never happened.

He glanced over at Maureen. She was still sleeping. He wanted her to notice him, so he thumped about the bed getting dressed. He closed his bureau drawer so it rasped shut. Maureen's eyelids were fluttering. Good. He'd have her up soon.

Robert trudged to the barn in the dark of the early autumn morning. The air was clean and cold. The three-quarter moon was dipping down towards the horizon, and the stars shone in stark relief. At five a.m. the cows were awake and ready to be milked, their udders full. Their body warmth filled the barn, along with the scent of hay and manure. He fastened the mechanical milkers to their teats, one by one, as he watched the pure, white milk being piped to the holding tank.

He was startled by a noise at the barn door. It was Jacob, slogging his way into the barn at 5:30 a.m. "Beat ya to it, son," Robert said, amused.

"Why didn't you tell me you were gonna milk? I coulda slept in on my Saturday," Jacob grumbled. "Didn't you go hunting last night?"

"No, not really. Wasn't havin' any luck, so I came

157

home early."

"Do you need some help? Since I'm here, already?"

"Nah, it's a one-person job. You know that. Go on back up to the house."

"Mom's up. She's makin' breakfast," said Jacob.

"Tell her I'll be over to the house when I'm done."

Robert finished up, still feeling exhausted but ready for breakfast nevertheless. As he entered the kitchen, he took off his boots at the door. "Morning, Honey," he said jauntily, though he felt the precise opposite.

"Good morning, sweetheart," Maureen said. "You're chipper today after a night of hunting. Usually you drag into the kitchen around noon."

"I wasn't having any luck at all last night, so I packed it in early, and came home," he said.

"That's not like you. Usually, you stay out 'til dawn."

"Well, sometimes things don't go the way you expected."

Maureen gave him a searching look which he ignored. He sipped his coffee, reached for the sugar jar, poured some in, and stirred it thoroughly. "Here's your breakfast," she said, as she placed a plate of eggs, toast, and bacon in front of him.

Maureen made Jacob a plate, then one for herself. The three sat in silence and ate. Jacob finished first, rose, and took his plate and empty glass to the kitchen sink. He left the kitchen for the central sitting room and slumped on the couch.

Maureen said in a low voice to Robert, "So, do you want to tell me what's going on?"

"Nothing, sweetie."

"Oh, come on."

"Well, okay." Robert gave a sheepish look to Maureen. "I went hunting over by the Quinn's house…"

Maureen's eyes sharpened and her mouth became taut. She held her breath.

"The long and the short of it, is I took a potshot at Mickey Quinn as he was getting out of his car. The shot struck his car and started a small fire. The fire was in his garage…"

"Oh, my God! You burned their house down?"

"I don't think so. Fire trucks were already on their way as I was escaping."

"But you don't know the extent of the damage, yet!"

"No."

"Thank God you didn't shoot him, or you'd be a murderer," she whispered fiercely, suddenly remembering that Jacob was in the next room.

Robert's mouth twitched. In shame, in regret, in embarrassment.

"My God! Robert! Where is the gun now?"

"In the cabinet, locked away, where it always is."

"Is it clean? Will it show that it's been fired?"

"Maureen, you're right. I've got to clean the gun!"

"Do it now, before anyone comes around here asking questions."

"You're right. I'll do it before the twins wake up."

"Hurry, Robert. There's no time to lose."

CHAPTER 32

After the last of the firefighters had left, Mickey went into his house. He headed straight for his living room, where he sank into the comforting depths of his leather couch. Clarisse found him there sitting in the dark.

"Don't you want the light on, sweetie?" she said.

"No. Sometimes I think better in the dark," he replied.

"What are you thinking about?"

"Who the hell would have the balls to take a shot at me."

Clarisse sat down tentatively in one of the side chairs alongside the couch. She wrapped her robe around her legs where it had gapped open. She wondered if the woman he had gotten pregnant had a husband or boyfriend that was extremely angry at him. It would serve him right.

Clarisse was achingly curious about the other woman and her circumstances and wished she could just ask Mickey openly about her.

"Who would have a motive?" asked Clarisse.

"Are you going to play girl-detective now?"

"Why not?" said Clarisse. "Don't they usually get the bad guy in the end?"

Mickey was silent for a long moment, stroking his cheek with his forefinger. He was thinking that it would be ironic if his only child would be born without a father, after all this time he had tried for fatherhood. His plan of getting Clarisse to adopt Darlene's child would never work, he saw now. He would have to get rid of Clarisse, probably divorce her. That was a pain in the ass, but the least worry, in the end.

"Actually, since you ask about motive, I can think about several people," said Mickey.

"You have that many enemies?"

"Nah, just disappointed business associates."

"Did you cheat these people?"

"Nah, they just got the short end of the stick."

"Why is that?"

"They ain't too sharp."

"Would they try to shoot you over a business dealing?"

"I didn't think so, at the time."

"Well, it must mean life or death to them."

Mickey slapped his thigh with the palm of his hand. "That's it! It's a matter of life or death to him." He turned to Clarisse. "You're a genius, babe! You just figured out who it was!"

"Who?"

"The farmer, Jaston!"

"Really?"

"Absolutely! That farm is life or death to him and his family! He's the one who'd try to kill me! Son-of-a-bitch!"

"Are you sure?"

"I'm sure. I'm so sure, I'm calling the police chief with my suspicions. I want the cops to arrest that son-of-a-bitch and throw him in jail!"

"You're sure it's the farmer, Mr. Jaston, and not

someone from your personal life?" asked Clarisse.

"What are you implying?" asked Mickey with a sudden sideways glance at Clarisse.

"Oh, nothing," said Clarisse, airily.

"Sounds like something to me," he growled.

"Just that everyone needs to keep their personal life in order...you know..."

"Sounds like someone has been snooping around, to me."

"Never mind."

Mickey gave her a long, hard, assessing stare, then reached for the phone. He dialed 911.

"Emergency. What's your emergency?"

"I'd like to speak to the police about who set the fire at my house and who took a shot at me a few hours ago. I'm positive that I know who did it, and there's no time to lose if you're gonna arrest him!"

"Sergeant Brooks here. Sorry to hear about the fire, Mr. Quinn. The man in charge of the overnight shift would be Lieutenant Tommy McMann. I'll transfer your call."

"Tommy! This is Michael Quinn. I'm calling about who set fire to my house and who took a shot at me just about two hours ago."

"Yeah. Heard about that one over the scanner. Could've been a doozy if it had gotten outta control, but our firefighters nipped that one out quick."

"Listen, I'm positive that the one who did this to me is that farmer, Robert Jaston," said Mickey.

"Now, come on, Mr. Quinn, I know you two have some bad blood between you, but we need a warrant to make an arrest," said Lieutenant McMann.

"I'm telling you, it's true!"

"We still need a warrant if we're gonna make an arrest, Mr. Quinn."

"Tommy, are you going to arrest Jaston for me or do I have to let your wife in on a secret or two?"

"Jeez, Mr. Quinn. I didn't know it mattered that much to you."

"It does. I am positive he's the son-of-a-bitch who tried to off me, not to mention set fire to my Cadillac and my house!"

"Well, we can question him. Can you go to the judge and get him to issue a warrant? The police department needs something to work with."

"I'll get my lawyer friend, Tobias Meachum, to work it out with the D.A.'s office!"

"That'll work."

"Okay then. Once the warrant issues, I expect you guys to make the arrest as soon as possible!"

"Will do."

"Not that it'll be any good. He will have destroyed any evidence by then."

"We'll see."

"Trust me, he will have. The man's no fool."

"Take care, Mr. Quinn. See ya around."

"Okay, Tommy. See ya." Mickey hung up the phone and looked over at Clarisse who was watching from her chair opposite him. She looked bleary-eyed from no sleep.

"Okay, babe. We can go to bed, now. Business is over for the night."

"That's my Mickey," she said. "Always setting the wheels in motion, even as you sleep."

"You better believe it, babe."

CHAPTER 33

Robert Jaston lifted his gun carefully out of the cabinet and placed it across his knees. He checked again to make sure that no bullets were left in the chamber. He then proceeded to methodically clean the inside and the outside of the rifle with his polishing cloth, going over each surface twice.

Trembling with fatigue, he stood up to place the gun back in its cabinet. There was a loud pounding on his front door. He managed to lock the cabinet before turning towards the door. "Maureen!" he called out. "Can you answer the door?"

Maureen trotted to the front room from the kitchen, wide-eyed. "Who could that be at six-thirty on a Saturday morning?" she whispered to Robert.

"Police! Open up!" came the muffled response.

"Oh my God!" whispered Maureen. "Did you clean the gun?"

"Just finished it," Robert whispered back. "Not to worry, my sweet. Now answer the door, please. And act calm."

Maureen cracked open the door a few inches. The cop shoved it open and strode inside. "I have a warrant for the arrest of Robert Jaston, ma'am. Is he here?"

"That would be me," said Robert, stepping forward, head held high. "Is that you, Officer Brooks? And Officer Lewis? But I want to know what this is all about."

"You'll find out soon enough, when you're charged at the station," said Officer Brooks gruffly, and seemingly embarrassed. "Now, come with us." He placed a pair of cuffs on Robert's wrists and began leading him out the front door. Robert twisted his head to look behind him and saw the faces of his wife and son in the doorway, wearing shock and despair.

The drive to the county jail was a blur. Robert was so tired. He had been awake the entire night, repeatedly seeing Mickey's car burst into flames, and then reliving his flight back to his truck on the dark road. The sound of sirens resounded in his sleeplessness. He rested his head on the back seat of the police car. He closed his eyes which were burning from lack of sleep.

"He's one cool customer," commented Officer Brooks. "Sleeping on the way to jail."

"Might as well catch his sleep now," said Officer Lewis. "Won't catch any sleep in the joint."

The police car drove up to the county jail. "Wake up, Sleeping Beauty! We've arrived at your castle," said Officer Lewis.

Robert opened his burning eyes. When the cop opened the rear car door, he got out, and followed them to the front door of the concrete building. The jail looked like a fortress. It had slit windows and a squat silhouette. No one was going to escape, and no one was going to burn this building down.

Robert's legs felt rubbery as he walked through the front door. He knew it was a lot easier walking in here than walking out.

The two cops walked on either side of him to the

front counter. It was a broad, formica counter, which almost hid the two women sitting behind it. "Marge," said the first cop, "we've got an intake for you."

"What are the charges?" asked Marge. She was a skinny, white-haired woman with a perennially suspicious look on her face.

"Attempted murder and arson," said Officer Brooks.

"What?" said Robert. "You gotta be kidding me!"

"Do I look like I kid around?" said Officer Brooks.

"I need to call my lawyer!" said Robert. "This is serious!"

"Damn right, it's serious, buddy. You're in deep shit."

"I need to call my lawyer this instant!"

"All in good time, buddy. First we gotta write up the charges, then we gotta take your mug shot, and so on."

"I didn't do any of this, whatever you say I did."

"That's what they all say."

"But I really didn't!"

"Tell it to the judge."

"Stand up straight for your mug shot," said Marge. The camera flashed. "Turn to the right." The camera flashed again. "The other side." The camera flashed yet again.

"Okay, he can go into holding cell 214. I'll need your watch, rings, money, wallet, any other valuables, belt, and shoes. I'll hold them for you until your release."

Robert felt a deep shame as he tendered his wallet,

his keys, his wedding ring, his watch, his belt, and his shoes. He stood there, holding up his jeans so they wouldn't slip down on him, embarrassing him further.

"This way," the cop said gruffly. Robert followed him down a long corridor that led to a steel door at the end. A guard, who looked like a bulldog, opened the steel door and took over escorting him to his cell.

Cell 214 was halfway down the line of cells. The guard unlocked the cell, unlocked Robert's handcuffs, and gave him a little shove into the cell. The cell door clanged shut behind Robert, and he had to face the fact that he was truly in jail.

"Hey!" he yelled. "Guard! Guard!"

But the guard was already gone.

"Shut up!" said the prisoner in the next cell.

"I got a question!"

"Go to hell!"

"When do I get to call my lawyer?"

"When they let you. Now shut the hell up!"

"Why do you have a hair across your ass?" asked Robert.

"Because the more trouble you make in here, the longer it is 'til ya get out, idiot!"

"How do you know?"

"I been in here a coupla times. It's worse each round."

Robert fell silent, wondering what his neighboring cellmate could have done to warrant multiple jailings.

"What're you in here for?" asked the neighboring cellmate.

"Attempted murder and arson. But I didn't do it."

"Of course not, buddy. It's all a set-up."

"What are you in here for?"

"Drug bust. They claim I was selling heroin and cocaine."

"Were you?"

"No way, man. It was all a set-up."

"So how do I get to call my lawyer?"

"They usually let people make their phone calls after lunch, at 1:00 o'clock. But today's a Saturday. Your lawyer won't be in the office today."

"Damn."

"Yeah. Weekend busts are a real drag, 'cause ya gotta wait for the lawyers to come back to work on Monday."

"Bummer," said Robert.

"So did you really try and smoke that guy?" asked the neighboring cellmate.

"No. I didn't. It's all a mistake. I didn't do anything."

"Okay, buddy. Whatever you say."

"I really didn't," said Robert, beginning to convince himself that it had all been a bad dream. Just a dream. *Life is just a dream.* So the song went. He went over to the narrow cot in his cell and laid down. The mattress was mildewed and lumpy and rested on rusty, metal springs. He shifted and the springs squealed. He couldn't get comfortable. But he was so bone-tired that his discomfort didn't matter. Soon, he was drifting off to sleep.

A scraping and clanging arose down the line. Robert began to surface from his sleep, like a swimmer striving to reach air. "Lunch" was the word repeatedly shouted by the guards. The lunch cart approached slowly, one wheel squeaking irregularly.

Robert's mouth began to salivate as he lay on his cot. It had been hours since he had eaten breakfast back at the farm. He groaned aloud as he thought of the farm. He had just jeopardized its status immeasurably by being arrested. As if things weren't delicate enough with the eminent domain looming over them.

The lunch cart stopped outside of his cell. A slot for a tray swung inwards, and a tray was shoved through. Robert was there to catch it. A bottled water rolled off jerkily from the plastic tray that now rested on the floor. Lunch was a wrapped white bread sandwich with a single slice of bologna. An apple shone dully on the plastic tray.

Robert ate quickly. Everything tasted surprisingly good to him. He ate the apple down to the core, then licked the juices off his fingers.

Soon the lunch cart reversed itself, this time collecting the trays and trash. Robert sat back on his cot to wait. He noticed the cement floor was grimy. He wondered how often the cells were cleaned. He wondered how often the jail got new mattresses. Hopefully, this one didn't have bedbugs, or nits, or fleas, or God-knows-what.

"Mr. Jaston, Cell 214, come with me," said a guard who had appeared at his cell door.

"What's going on?"

"Time for your phone call," said the guard with a smirk. The guard fiddled with his ring of keys, finally unlocking the steel door and then escorted him down the hallway.

They ended up in the general holding area which had a wall of pay phones. "Here's a dollar's worth of coins. Use them wisely. That's all you get."

Robert Jaston pocketed all the coins but one, and called the operator. "Collect call to Maureen Jaston, please," he said. There was a pause.

"Hello?" Maureen answered with a question in her voice.

"Maureen, it's me. Say you'll take a collect call from me."

"Do you accept the collect call charges, ma'am?" interrupted the operator.

"Yes! I do!"

"Maureen, I'm in the county jail. I need a lawyer who can get me out of here as soon as possible. Can you call Anna?"

"Sure I can. I'll call her at her home. I'm sure she'll do work on the weekends. She's a trooper."

"Thanks, sweetheart. You're the best."

"Don't worry about things while you're gone. Jacob has everything well in hand."

"He's a good boy."

"Yes, he is. And the girls are being good, too. We just have to get you home as soon as possible."

CHAPTER 34

"Lucky for you," said Anna to Robert Jaston from the opposite side of his jail cell, "the cops forgot to recite your Miranda rights to you when they arrested you."

"What are those?"

"You know, that you have the right to remain silent; that anything you say may be used against you; that you have the right to a lawyer, and so on."

"Oh, all that stuff they say on the cop shows on TV," he said.

"Yeah."

"So what does that mean to me?"

"That the arrest is going to be thrown out because it was illegal."

"Really?"

"Really." Anna put her left hand against the cold steel bars. "In the meantime, we're going to get you out by posting a bond for you. I will go speak to the bail bondsman."

"Anna, I can't thank you enough. Especially for coming in on the weekend for me."

"Hey, that's what we lawyers are for! We have to make ourselves useful sometimes, huh?" She turned to look down the long corridor. "I guess I'd better get back to the front office and get the paperwork started."

***

Wearing his street clothes again felt like an unimaginable luxury to Robert as he climbed into the front passenger side of Anna Ebert's little green Escort. He felt very conspicuous as he stared out of the front windshield. Probably all of Longbottom knew by now that he had been arrested and thrown in jail. He didn't want to end up named in the police log of the Longbottom Tribune for all to read.

Anna was back in the courthouse, straightening out some last minute paperwork. He wondered what was taking her so long. He wanted to be at home, and he desperately needed a shower. He stunk. He knew it because he could smell himself. He wondered how bad he smelled to other people.

Robert found out when Anna got in the car and cracked the windows open an inch on either side, despite the cool air. She hadn't said anything, and he was grateful for her discretion.

"I didn't do it, you know," he said.

"Okay."

"Really."

"It's okay. I always take my client's word for something," she said.

"Good," said Robert. He was of the opinion that if he could convince his lawyer that he was innocent, then his lawyer would convince the world that he was innocent.

"In the meantime, no more deer hunting for you, Mr. Jaston."

"Of course not."

"That would be seen as unduly provocative."

"Yeah. I guess so."

"Good. Just so we understand each other."

There was silence between them as they navigated the country roads that led from the county jail back to Longbottom.

Robert watched the houses and businesses that lined the road. He couldn't help thinking of his farm.

"You know my family and I only have another three months 'til we have to be out."

"I know," said Anna. "If only we could get a break in the case somehow. We've been pushing and pushing and we haven't had that breakthrough yet."

"But did we ever really have a chance if that Supreme Court case was against us from the start?"

"Yes, because at the heart of it, it's a corruption case. And in corruption cases, your opponents get sent to prison."

"Except in this case, where the victim of the corruption is the one who goes to jail for the weekend," said Robert bitterly. "How come everything seems upside-down and inside-out?"

"Well, there you actually did catch a break, in the going to jail part."

"I hardly think so."

"Believe me, you did. I think those cops deliberately left out your Miranda warnings so that the arrest would be invalid. And let you off the hook."

"And why would they do that?" asked Robert.

"It's possible they didn't really want to arrest you."

"Why not?"

"Maybe they didn't think you had done it."

"Well, I hadn't."

"There you go. And they probably knew from the outset that you weren't the one."

"If they thought that, then why arrest me anyway?"

Anna took her eyes off the road to turn her head and look him directly.

"Robert, your father was a selectman in his day. He must have told you how everything is political, including who the police arrest, and who they don't arrest that deserved it, and including who has a warrant issued on them on scant grounds."

"Yeah. That's the part he hated. That's why he gave up his seat after two terms."

"Well then, you know. I think your arrest was made to satisfy someone, probably Mickey Quinn, but also deliberately botched in order to help you. You have secret friends and sympathizers that you're not aware of." She smiled at him and he looked away.

Robert hated lying to Anna, but he felt that he had no choice. He needed her righteous indignation fueling his defense and shepherding his land case.

Just then his farm came into view, pretty as a postcard. He grinned at the sight. "Home, sweet home, at least a little bit longer!"

CHAPTER 35

After the fire, the morning broke into a clear day. The geese outside Mickey Quinn's house had flown south for the season, so the only irregular sound was the occasional wind gust clawing at the house. Yet both Mickey and Clarisse lay asleep on the king-sized bed upstairs until noon when Clarisse woke abruptly to the sound of the phone ringing.

"Hello?' she mumbled.

"Mrs. Quinn? I'm calling to find out if you have any interest in buying or selling a vacation timeshare?"

Clarisse hung up the phone and reached over to shake Mickey awake. "Sweetie, time to get up."

"Darlene, honey…" he muttered into his pillow.

With a sharp intake of breath, Clarisse stiffened. He had gone over to the other side, to the other woman, in his dreams. Which meant he had probably gone over to her in his heart. She felt a quick pain in her chest, under her heart. She withdrew her hand from Mickey and got off the bed from her side.

Clarisse dressed while Mickey still lay on the bed. Her thoughts were swirling in her head as she went downstairs to make the coffee. As the coffee percolated, Mickey came shuffling down the stairs, still in his sleeping shorts, his blond hair ruffled.

"Mornin' sunshine," said Clarisse.

"Spare me the morning cheer," said Mickey. "I had a rough night last night, as you might recall."

"Poor baby."

Mickey stopped in his tracks and looked her in the eye. "And what's going on with you, huh? Why the sarcasm?"

Here it comes, thought Clarisse. Do I let on that I know? She was silent a long moment, while Mickey waited, leaning against the doorjamb.

Clarisse took a deep breath and said, "Last night you said 'Darlene honey' in your sleep. I want to know what that's all about, and who she is."

Mickey's blue eyes blazed hotter. "You really want to know?"

"Yeah."

"She's the woman who's having my child. My long dreamed-of child. At last."

Clarisse choked on her coffee, then sputtered. She was incapable of a response, being so full of contradictory emotions. On one hand, she was jealous; on the other hand, she was perversely glad for him that he was getting what he so badly wanted. She was angry at him for having cheated on her, yet she sympathized with someone who would keep on trying for their dream child. He was just a complicated, persistent bastard, who would stop at nothing to get his way. Finally, she said, "So where does that leave me?"

Mickey said, pokerfaced, "That's something I've been meaning to talk to you about."

"That's nice. To let me in on it now."

"I was going to have to tell you sooner or later. Better sooner, I suppose."

"So lay it on me."

"Originally, I was thinking that you and I would adopt the child of Darlene and raise the child as our own."

Clarisse's eyes widened at the thought.

"But Darlene would never go for that. She is insisting that she, and she alone, will raise that child."

"So where do you come in?"

"I intend to sue for joint custody of the child, and have the child at least part-time," said Mickey.

"I'm sure Darlene will be forever angry at you if you do that."

"Or, I follow another plan."

"Which is?"

"I'd rather not get into it right now."

"I'm sure it's another hare-brained scheme if it ever was," said Clarisse.

"When are my ideas ever half-assed? Huh?" Mickey suddenly looked spit-fire mean. "Do I ever do anything half-assed?"

"No," admitted Clarisse.

"Alright, then. And just you remember it."

Clarisse turned away towards the kitchen sink and began rinsing her coffee cup, if only to avoid the intensity of Mickey's stare. "Since I'm dressed, I'll go out and get the morning newspaper," she said.

The newspaper headline said it all: "Dairy Farmer Jailed for Attempted Murder, Arson" and showed the mug shots of Robert Jaston.

"Looks like the cops arrested the farmer like you wanted them to," said Clarisse.

She tossed the newspaper down on the coffee table

by the blue leather couch in the living room. "Come read the details of the article."

Mickey scowled as he walked from the kitchen to the living room, still in his sleeping shorts. "I can't stand that local rag. I didn't know there were any reporters here last night."

"There probably weren't," said Clarisse, "but they found out soon enough."

"Read me the best parts," said Mickey.

Clarisse picked up the newspaper and began reading about the fire in their garage and in their Cadillac.

"Skip that part," commanded Mickey.

Clarisse began reading about the dawn raid on the farm which netted Robert Jaston as the suspect and how he was transported to the county jail for booking.

Mickey grinned hugely and rubbed his as-of-yet-unshaven jaw.

Clarisse concluded with the fact that Robert Jaston was out of jail, on bond set at $50,000, and that he was back on his dairy farm.

"$50,000! Shit! That ain't jack-shit! All he had to put up was 10% of that, which was $5,000! Any half-wit can come up with that kind of money!" fumed Mickey. "Wonder how he got that easy bond."

"Isn't it enough that you got him arrested?" asked Clarisse. "And his face splashed all over the front of the newspaper?"

"It's a start. What I really want is him out of commission. That would make this whole casino development so much easier."

179

"So this whole vendetta against him is really just about his land?"

"Of course it is, babe. What did you think it was about?"

Clarisse was silent, thinking. As far as she was concerned, what was happening to the Jastons was cruel and unjust. Maybe, in some small way, she could remedy that.

Surreptitiously, that is. If Mickey ever found out she was working against him, he would kill her. Literally. But working against Mickey would provide a certain poetic justice to the fact that he had betrayed her with another woman. However, she would have to be exceedingly careful in how she proceeded. If she dared.

CHAPTER 36

"It's a good thing my parents have both passed away," said Maureen as she handed a cup of steaming coffee to Robert. He was seated in his usual chair at the round, wooden kitchen table, with their three wide-eyed children in attendance. "They'd never get over the shame of having a jailbird for a son-in-law."

Fourteen year old Jacob winced at those words, and turned his big black eyes, so like his father's, to look for his father's reaction. Robert Jaston merely smiled wryly at those words and said nothing.

The twin girls leaned in on the table on their elbows, uncharacteristically silent, wide-eyed, and watching their mother for cues.

"Imagine my shock at seeing the morning newspaper, showing your face. Your face, staring out at me, looking guilty as sin, thank you, on the front page!" Maureen's normally pale complexion became pink, until it seemed to match her auburn hair.

"Now, Maureen," said Robert. "Don't get yourself so worked up about it. I agree it's shameful to be on the front page of the newspaper as the latest arrest, but then it was equally painful for me to go public and run for political office. All of it is a violation of my privacy."

"Running for political office is not a bit like being arrested!" said Maureen heatedly.

"I'm not about to get into a philosophical argument with you about the merits of one over the other. It's time for me to milk the cows. Jacob, I hear you did a fine job while I was away. Want to come with me now?"

"Sure, Dad," said Jacob, glad to be escaping the explosive atmosphere in the kitchen.

Robert and his son quietly left the kitchen to walk down the stone and gravel path to the barn.

"Your mother is overly sensitive to public opinion," said Robert.

Their boots slashed against the tall grass that tilted inward at the edges of the path. They both looked down with every step to where they placed their feet.

"I know," said Jacob, finally. "You should have seen her after you were arrested. She was like a crazy person. She was crying and even swearing. I never, ever heard her swear before."

"Huh," said Robert. "I never would have thought that of her."

"Finally, she stopped crying, and called your lawyer, that Anna Ebert-lady. After talking to her, she was a lot calmer."

"Good."

"The twins have been good, surprisingly," said Jacob. "Layla and Shaina have been acting as though someone died, which means, on their best behavior."

"Well, at least that's been a help to your mother."

They reached the barn door and pulled it open. As the work began, the talk between them ceased. Only the occasional mooing of a cow broke the silence.

Robert could see that Jacob was itching to ask him more. He thought about donning a stern face just to forestall the inevitable questions, but he had a vision of himself physically pushing away his son with his demeanor, just as his father had often done to him. His father had been kind but had been an old-school, strict, upright New Englander. He had rarely unbent his ramrod back to let loose a hearty laugh, and had, to Robert's knowledge, never shed a tear.

Jacob finished with his half of the chores before his father. He came to stand next to Robert, waiting. Robert could feel the questions pressing against him. He finished up his chores methodically, averting his face from Jacob's.

"Dad..." Jacob burst out at last.

Robert turned his ink-black eyes towards Jacob, who stood an inch shorter than him still. He waited.

"What was it like in jail?"

"Not good."

"Come on, Dad, tell me some details..."

Robert hitched his thumbs into the loops at the waist of his jeans and grimaced.

"I was in a tiny cell, stinking and grimy, next door to a low-life drug dealer who was a regular at the jail."

Robert watched Jacob stare at the barn floor as he absorbed this information.

"Did anyone rough you up?"

"No. They don't do that in this day and age. At least not to a middle-aged white guy like me. Somebody else may not have been so lucky."

Jacob continued to stare at the barn floor. "But I had to turn over my wallet, my keys, my watch, my belt, so my pants were falling down on me, and my wedding ring. That hurt the most. I haven't taken off my wedding ring, ever, since the day your mother and I married. To have to take off the wedding ring because I was accused of a crime was the worst."

"Dad, did you, did you do anything, bad?"

"No, son. I was out deer hunting, and things turned a bit crazy."

"What do you mean?"

Robert realized he had already said too much. "I was out deer hunting, and the next thing I knew, sirens were blowing and cop cars were speeding up the road. I decided the best thing to do was for me to get out of there."

"The newspaper said there was a fire at the Quinn house," said Jacob.

"Uh huh."

"You didn't have anything to do with that fire, did you, Dad?"

Robert looked at Jacob, who was staring at him intently. This was the moment of truth. Or not.

"No, I didn't," said Robert, looking Jacob directly in the eye. Robert held Jacob's gaze for a long, unblinking moment.

"I believe you, Dad," said Jacob finally, letting his squared-up shoulders relax.

Robert felt enormous relief. Jacob would now be unerringly on his side. He would have to likewise convince Maureen that he had meant no harm, that he had merely acted out of a foolish frustration. And it was true.

I hadn't meant to set the fire, he thought. I had simply taken a pot-shot at Mickey Quinn out of sheer, pent-up anxiety over my land being taken away from me. That was different than a specific intent to kill. Murder involves actual intent to kill someone. I'm not a murderer, not me, he said to himself. I'm just protecting my farm against all these people who are ganging up on me. I just have to keep my thoughts straight, and everything will work out in the end...

CHAPTER 37

Clarisse watched Mickey as he dressed for the day at his pub. He had chosen a slim-fitted dress shirt, left unbuttoned at the neck, where some golden chest hairs curled up and out. Followed by suit pants and suit jacket, the jacket to be set aside in his office as soon as he arrived.

Bit much for just a pub, she noted. He was dressing as if he was the business tycoon of a major business enterprise. But, then again, that's exactly what he hoped to be when this casino came into town, she realized. Then he'd have it all: his big business and his first child. But not with her. She swallowed, tasting the bitterness on her tongue.

"I'm going to be taking your Subaru to work today, since the Cadillac is damaged from the fire," he announced.

"Oh," said Clarisse. That was going to put a definite crimp in her plans.

"You weren't going anywhere today, were you?"

Clarisse thought fast. "Just my book club, at the town library. I could call the town cab to take me. I hate to miss it since it only meets once a month."

"Okay. Here's money for the cab." He tossed a twenty onto the bed.

"Thanks, Mickey. I happen to be low on cash."

"No problem." He leaned over to kiss her proprietarily on the lips. "See ya later."

He turned to leave their bedroom. She heard him clomping down the stairs, through the family room, to the door that led to the garage. She listened to the garage door opener whine and the Subaru engine rumble. A moment later he was gone.

Clarisse dialed the phone number for Russo's Cab Co. They agreed to pick her up in half an hour. Next Clarisse took out her cell phone and dialed Anna Ebert's phone number. "Is Attorney Ebert in the office today?"

"Yes, she is," said Trudy. "May I ask who's calling?"

"I need to speak to Attorney Ebert about something confidential, and let's just say that my name is CeeCee."

"CeeCee as in Cecelia?"

"Yes."

"Do you have a last name?"

"I'd rather not give it out, if you don't mind."

"Alright. Here's Attorney Ebert on the line."

Clarisse spoke in hushed tones to Attorney Ebert for several minutes.

Next, Clarisse went to the kitchen and removed some heavy, little-used pots and pans from the bottom cabinet. Bending over, she flushed rosy with exertion. Just then, the phone rang. Clarisse bumped her head on the cabinet, trying to get up to answer the phone. On the third ring, she answered it. "Hello?"

"Hey babe."

"What's up, Mickey?"

"It occurred to me that I shoulda given ya a ride into town. Want me to swing back and get ya?"

"Don't worry. I already called the cab company.

They're already on their way."

"Alright. You're sure?"

"I'm sure."

"Okay. Bye."

Clarisse hung up the phone and sagged against the kitchen wall. That Mickey Quinn had an uncanny ability to intuit when she was up to something. It was almost like he was a mind-reader.

She shook off her goose bumps and went back over to the stack of pots and pans. She reached inside the cabinet and took out an envelope. She opened it and saw that the papers inside were there and intact. She smiled. This was going to create a firestorm.

***

Russo's cab dropped Clarisse off in front of the town library, off of the town common. Clarisse gave a quick glance to see if anyone she recognized was out and about. The town common was where all the town gossips went for lunch at the Tip Top Café, which was run by a man and his wife, and his former wife. The threesome was itself a source of gossip and speculation. Across the common was the Coffee Connection, for the younger, hipper crowd, who hung around for hours at a time with their laptops. Between them, not a sparrow peeped but somebody noticed and commented on it.

Clarisse walked casually towards the town library, with a large, hot-pink tote bag slung over her shoulder, in addition to her purse. She walked into the library and headed straight towards the copy machine.

She took out the large manila envelope that belonged to Mickey and began to copy the papers within pertaining to Darlene Bundt. When she was finished, she was careful to place the originals in the manila envelope exactly the way they were, back in the tote bag. She was also careful to keep her copies folded and separate, in her purse.

Clarisse casually stepped away from the copier and began to wander amongst the stacks of books. She began amongst the newest novels but realized they were inappropriate for her purposes. She continued on to the section containing the classic novels, but they looked well-worn and perhaps too popular. She kept wandering: biographies, history, geography, popular sciences.... Perhaps geography. Pick some completely obscure volume of a totally obscure country or region. That would do.

Hmmm. Madagascar? Guam? Siberia? Liberia? The rainforests of Brazil? Clarisse picked the book about Siberia off of the book shelf and began to thumb through it.

If Mickey ever found out what she was about to do, she might as well be banished to the far reaches of Siberia, if she wasn't already stone dead. Her eye swerved onto a photo of reindeer hitched to a sled. Clarisse smiled. On the other hand, it would be like a well-deserved Christmas gift to some folks who were currently hurting badly. Sometimes there just needed to be justice in this world, she thought, feeling a stab of righteousness swell her chest.

Don't get ahead of yourself, girl, she reminded

herself.

One careful step at a time.

Clarisse took several glances around her to make sure no one was watching her, where she stood in the book stacks. Then she slipped a single piece of paper that was folded into thirds like a business letter, and placed it between the middle pages of the book. Glancing around once more, she shelved the book.

Clarisse reached into her purse and took out a small pad of paper and a pen. She wrote the title of the book, *The Severe Beauty of Siberia,* along with its Dewey decimal system number, indicating its shelf position in the stacks. Satisfied, she walked out of the aisle and continued on to the elevator to the second floor. She was just in time for her book club, which was discussing *The Buddha in the Attic.* In fact it was her turn to lead the discussion about the book. Clarisse put the pad of paper and pen back in her purse. She reached into her large, hot-pink tote bag and pulled out the book, which she admired for its small, tidy presentation. It had been an unusual read.

After the book discussion, Clarisse wandered down the stairs to the first floor, where she returned her copy of the Buddha book. She began to wander the stacks in search of another good read or two. Casually, she checked those books out at the counter, then placed them in her tote bag. She walked outside, feeling the fresh air brush her face. People were walking in and out of the front door of the library, so she walked off to one side, and dialed Attorney Ebert on her cell phone.

"Anna Ebert here."

"It's CeeCee again."

"And?"

"I dropped it off in the library. I chose a book called the *The Severe Beauty of Siberia*, and its stack number is GEO185.247. It's on the right side, opposite the copy machine, under the second window. It's a tall, yellow book."

"Great. I can't thank you enough. I'll walk over there in half an hour, if you think you'll be gone," said Anna.

"I'll be gone. As soon as I hang up with you, I'm going over to the Tip Top Café, and from there, I'll go home at my leisure."

"Sounds like a plan."

"Attorney Ebert?"

"Yes?"

"My husband...oh, never mind. Let's just say that I think you're a hero."

"Thanks. I am. A little bit. But do you realize that the real hero is you? Enjoy the Tip Top," Anna said before hanging up her end of the phone call.

She was afraid this CeeCee would get too emotional and make a partial confession, which could jeopardize both of them, if, and this was a big if, either of their phones were being tapped. You just never knew.

Now, to make her way over to the library to retrieve that paper!

CHAPTER 38

Anna Ebert hung up from the cell phone call and felt both excitement and trepidation.

She rose from her chair and walked into the front reception room where Trudy sat, laboring over a complicated real estate closing statement. Trudy was chewing gum loudly and periodically blowing small bubbles from her bubblegum. Anna preferred that Trudy ditch the gum, and had suggested it on several occasions, but Trudy claimed it helped her concentrate. As Trudy blew her latest bubble, a lopsided blue one, Anna rolled her eyes to herself.

"I'm heading over to the library, Trudy."

"Okay," said Trudy. "When will you be back?"

"I'm not sure."

"Okay. But you've got a four o'clock appointment with Nellie Fester, remember…a worker's compensation case."

"That's right. Thanks for reminding me."

Anna exited the office and descended the flight of narrow stairs that led to the front foyer of the building. She pushed open the heavy glass door and was greeted with the low groan of an eighteen-wheeler truck making its way around the town common in low gear, along with its exhaust. She grimaced, trying to hold her breath so the exhaust would not go deep into her lungs. Those poor, frail trees growing on the common, she thought. How do they keep growing in the face of all this spewing on them day in and day out?

She began walking the block and a half from her office to the town library. The day's weather was moderate. Some silvery clouds scudded across the pale blue sky, but there was no sign of rain. Some of the trees had begun to turn scarlet and yellow and orange, which contrasted beautifully with the vibrant evergreens. She really should get out more, she thought. It was a pity she was shut in the office every day.

Anna made an abrupt right turn, as the sidewalk led to the library entrance.

She walked briskly up to the automatic doors, which hissed as they slid open. She passed through and went straight to the stacks where she began to read the topic labels on the end of each tall bookcase.

When she got to the geography section, she slowed down and went between the stacks. She reached into her suit jacket pocket and took out a slip of paper. Referring to it every few moments, she slowly made her way up the aisle until she got to the section of numbers that corresponded. At last, she spotted the oversized, yellow book titled *The Severe Beauty of Siberia*. Trembling, she took it off the shelf and held it in her arms. She began to leaf through the book and, halfway through, a paper tumbled out onto the floor. She immediately stooped over to retrieve it. She plopped the book on Siberia to one side, and clutched the paper.

Still trembling, Anna opened the folded paper and looked at it. She smiled broadly. She began to chuckle quietly. Here was the break she had been hoping for!

CHAPTER 39

Mickey Quinn got a call from a "Restricted" number on his cell phone. He knew who it was. The cop he had hired "for private duty service" to tap into Clarisse's cell phone off the record was calling him with some news.

"Hey."

"Hey."

"Whatcha got?"

"First phone tip I got that ain't entirely kosher. Or boring. Subject contacted E., and after a phone call between them, arranged a drop in the public library."

"Of what?"

"Don't know. Wasn't able to get there in time to intercept the drop. When I pulled into the parking lot, E. was walking out of the library already."

"Any idea of what it could be, from the phone call?"

"No idea, but subject indicated to E. that it could be the 'break' she needed."

"Shit." Mickey felt the first emissions of sweat trickle down from his armpits into the fabric of his polo shirt. "You know we're going to have to get the thing - tape, video, or document - whatever it is, and destroy it."

"Yeah."

"You up to it?"

"Maybe. Depends if E.'s place's got an alarm or a safe inside."

"When will you find out?"

"Soon."

"You'll let me know if you're gonna do it?"

"Sure."

"And if not?" asked Mickey.

"Guess you'll have to turn to Plan B, 'cause I ain't doin' no Watergate here."

"Fair enough." Mickey touched his cell phone to end the call.

***

That night, Mickey drove home in a cold rage. He pictured his hands around the slender, white throat of Clarisse, squeezing the life out of her gradually, as she slowly went limp before him. He smiled grimly at the thought. It was two o'clock in the morning, with few other cars on the road, yet he rigidly maintained the speed limit. If he could control his speed, then he could control his anger. By controlling his anger, he wouldn't kill her. At least not yet. At least not in haste, in rage, with thoughtlessness, in a manner that was sure to land him in prison for years to come. If he was going to kill her, he would do it in a thoughtful way, a way that would leave no trace, a way that would leave him clear to marry his next wife, like Darlene, for example, who was carrying his child. If Clarisse were conveniently dead, he could marry Darlene without any complications like having to go through a divorce and reach a settlement on property. His property for the most part. As if Clarisse had brought anything to the marriage other that her cute, tight, little ass. Her cute, tight, disloyal, little ass. The bitch.

He felt the cold rage settle in his belly behind his

solar plexus, where it would fuel his energy level for days and weeks to come. As he maneuvered the dark streets of Longbottom, he remembered that she would most likely be asleep when he arrived home, so he would not have to confront her. Good. He did not want to talk to her. Ever again.

As he swung the Subaru into the driveway, he glanced up to the second floor of their home. The bedroom light was off. Very good. He shut off the engine and closed the garage door. He walked inside the house, stood by the door and listened. There was only the ticking of the kitchen clock and the humming of the refrigerator to be heard. He took off his shoes in the entranceway and picked them up in his left hand. In his stocking feet, he headed up the creaking wooden stairs and turned down the hallway towards the master bedroom.

Clarisse was sleeping on her back, her head turned to one side. Through the many-paned window, a sliver of moonlight cast an arc across her cheek and forehead.

There she sleeps, Mickey thought, as if she weren't guilty of deception and disloyalty. She sleeps the sleep of the innocent. But I know better. All in due time.

Chapter 40

A dusty, dented, black truck drove into the alleyway behind Anna Ebert's office slightly after three a.m. Two scruffy white men, both dressed in all black, emerged from the truck. One of them pulled a rope from his backpack. He flung it upwards, so that it caught the fire escape scaffolding. The stairs of the fire escape screeched as they were pulled down to street level. Startled, the men scanned the alley for unwelcome witnesses, but there were none. The two men silently and swiftly climbed the fire escape stairs to the landing at the rear of Anna Ebert's office. The second man produced a crowbar and began prying open the wooden door. With little effort, they were inside.

Two days earlier, one of the men, who went by the name of Willard Dupre, had gone to Anna's office on an appointment. Mr. Dupre had gone to have his will written up, at long last. As he had explained it then, he was fifty-five, officially a senior citizen, and had never had his last will and testament drawn.

Actually, he had been there to case out the joint. He had discreetly looked around the front waiting room, glad that Trudy was busy on the computer. He had eyed the ceiling and walls, but he had seen no evidence of any alarm system or surveillance apparatus. Looked to be a distinctly low-tech operation, here, he thought.

When he had entered Anna's office, he had been careful to maintain eye contact with her while still checking out the room. No safe, he noted. Back door behind her, in her office, was wooden. Probably led to the back entranceway. No way he could ask, he had thought to himself, bemusedly.

Smiling pleasantly, he had signed the Attorney/Client agreement with the name Willard Dupre and had thought how the will would be for naught since that wasn't his name. Oh, well. Business expense. Expensive wallpaper. And what did he care, when Mr. Quinn would reimburse him for all his costs?

Now that he and his partner were inside, they turned on their flashlights. This operation had to be quick since the office was on the town common and could conceivably be spotted by someone driving by and noticing lights within. Willard began scanning all the papers on the desk. He knew he had to find something that had to do with the Jastons. But Mr. Quinn hadn't been specific. Was it a paper? A tape? A video? Looking for a piece of unknown evidence in a lawyer's office was a nearly impossible task. His frustration began to rise. How did you know when you had found it? He turned to his partner.

"Find anything?"

"Nah."

"Where'd you look?"

"In the logical place, the Jaston folder in the file cabinet."

"This operation sucks. We'll never find it."

"No kidding."

"You know that if we don't find nothing, we're supposed to trash the place."

"Really?"

"Explicit instructions of Mr. Q. himself."

"Huh," said the other man wonderingly. "He got a grudge against this person?"

"Sure does," said Willard. "Says this here lawyer's been a thorn in his side for a long time, deserves to have her office trashed."

"Wow," the other man chuckled. "Guess we get to have some fun!" Then he reached into the file cabinet, grabbed some files, and dumped their contents into a heap on the floor. He reached into the next drawer and repeated the process.

"Just hurry up. We gotta get outta here soon."

"Just showing my respect for the legal profession."

"You're a crazy sum 'bitch."

"Yep, you got that right!"

As the other man continued to scatter files hither and yon, Willard prowled the office looking for nooks and crannies to plant a listening device or two in the office. He decided on the inside of one of the drawers of Anna's desk and, for the other one, the underside of a shelf on the tall wooden bookcase. They hadn't turned up anything in their search tonight, but one never knew what a well-timed conversation might soon reveal.

CHAPTER 41

Anna Ebert had decided to make a delicate telephone call from the sanctuary of her parents' home. She no longer trusted her office phone or her cell phone for any truly personal matters. In fact she found herself talking to her clients in a more circumspect manner over the office phone and arranging to meet them at their homes for the really delicate aspects of their cases.

Ever since her office had been burglarized, she had been feeling personally harassed. The morning of the discovery, Anna had walked into her office and yelled, "Holy shit!" at the sight of the papers strewn everywhere.

"Trudy!" she had bellowed, whirling around.

Trudy had come bounding in. "Oh my God! Anna! Who would do this?"

Anna had been silent as she contemplated the answer. She had had a pretty good idea who was behind it all, if not the actual perpetrators, but, of course, no proof. She decided against reporting this matter to the local police because they might be tangled up in it. Now she understood how the Jastons felt: singled out, betrayed, and persecuted for standing up for themselves.

But secrets usually revealed themselves when exposed to the light of day, she mused. And that was exactly what she intended to do.

She stood in her parents' bedroom, in front of her mother's bureau, with its sheer, lace runner covering the top, and a central oval mirror lying flat with colored bottles of perfume catching the light from the window. The old-fashioned princess telephone lay in its cradle at the far end of the bureau. She quietly picked up the receiver and began to dial.

"Hello? May I please speak to the editor, Steve Ballast?" She was put on hold.

The Longbottom Tribune was a newspaper of longstanding tradition. It had been in print for more than one hundred years. It was not known for its cutting edge journalism, but it enjoyed a relationship as a sister-newspaper with a larger regional newspaper. Together, the papers covered around one hundred thousand people. Its office was in the next town over, Orangeville.

A secretary came on the line. "What are you calling about?"

"It's a controversial story he will be interested in," said Anna. She was put on hold again.

Suddenly, he was there. "Steve Ballast." He sounded impatient.

"Hi, Steve, it's Anna Ebert. I've got an update on the Jaston recall situation. Last you covered him, he'd gone to jail. Well, some critical evidence has come up, and it's definitely newsworthy. Can I come it to your newsroom and see you?"

"Sure."

"Now?"

"Sure."

"See you in a bit, then." Anna gently placed the receiver back in its cradle. She sat down on the edge of her parents' bed, feeling the enormity of what she was about to do. She took a deep breath. It was now or never.

From her parents' bedroom she walked down the hallway to the kitchen. Her mother was standing at the kitchen sink, preparing lunch. "Where are you going?" asked Anna's mother.

"Out," replied Anna.

"Well, don't forget your coat. It looks like rain."

"Yes, mother," said Anna, irritated. She was how old now?

"Drive carefully in the rain, dear."

"Okay." Anna shrugged into her raincoat as she exited the front door. She got into her green Ford Escort and backed out of her parents' driveway. She turned to the right and drove down the tree-lined street. A drizzle coated her windshields, front and back, with a silver film. She bent down to turn the radio on to a better station. She didn't notice the nondescript truck that eased out from the curb and began to follow her.

Anna was preoccupied with what she was going to tell Steve Ballast. Therefore she wasn't watching her rear view mirror. The truck, a dirty black, with no logo and a crooked front fender, was following her very closely. She came to a stop sign, as did the truck behind her. Traffic was clear, so she proceeded forward. So did the truck, so fast, that it rammed into her car from behind.

"What the hell?" screamed Anna. She put her the gear into park and jumped out of her car in a rage. "What the hell are you guys doing, driving like that?" she yelled, standing outside her driver door.

Suddenly, she realized the driver was Willard

Dupre. He was staring back at her with an unreadable expression. His brown eyes were narrowed and fixed upon her, as if she were prey, she realized with a nasty shock. Suddenly, everything that had happened to her fell into place. She began to shake. She turned, jumped back into her car, rammed the engine into drive and drove off with a roar. Her rear fender dangled onto the road, setting off random sparks against the asphalt.

The black truck chased her car, ramming it from behind every so often, as they sped down the main highway, which was mostly empty of houses and businesses on this stretch between Longbottom and Orangeville.

If I can just get to the main drag of Orangeville, thought Anna, I'll make it. She ran through a yellow light at a wide intersection, hoping no one was coming. The truck followed, going through a red light. A police car started its siren and gave chase. Great, thought Anna. Now a whole caravan is following me. She pulled a sharp right turn without warning, tires screeching, and the truck and police car followed clumsily. Now she was in the downtown of Orangeville, and cars full of people on either side of the road were at a standstill, watching the chase, openmouthed, enthralled.

The Longbottom Tribune office was at the end of the block on the left. It was housed in a historically significant building, constructed of New Hampshire granite, and had the look of a fortress. A four-sided clock tower topped the building with an enormous working clock that chimed the hours.

As Anna rushed her car into the handicapped spot

in front of the Tribune building, the clock tower began a sonorous chiming of the hour. She had no time to lose. Their fates hung in the balance. Anna grabbed her purse and ran up the stone steps of the building to the heavy wooden doors.

Willard Dupre was a few steps behind her. Running behind both of them were the two cops, shouting at both of them to stop. Anna flung open the heavy wooden door, and raced up the marble steps to the second floor, where the newspaper offices were housed.

"Steve! Steve! Steve Ballast!" Anna screamed in the foyer. She burst into the newspaper general office. "Steve!" she screamed again. Heads in the newsroom instantly swiveled in her direction. "I've got a story for Steve, and I'm being chased!"

A moment later, Willard Dupre burst into the newsroom, followed by the two cops. Everyone in the newsroom was on high alert.

"You two are both under arrest for speeding and for evading an officer," gasped the first officer, coming to a standstill next to Willard Dupre and nodding his head in Anna's direction.

"Officer, I've got important business with the Longbottom Tribune," Anna announced loudly, so everyone in the newsroom could hear. "Arrest me after I speak to the editor."

"Lady, we don't arrest by appointment."

Steve Ballast stepped forward, his hand raised in a conciliatory gesture. "Gentlemen, officers, hold off for a few minutes, please. This lady had an appointment to speak with me about something very important. And I suspect it is indeed important if she's been chased on her way to this office." He cocked his head to one side atop his thin, 6'4" frame, taking in Anna's harried appearance and Willard Dupre's presence. "I need to talk to her for a few minutes. Then she's yours."

Anna gave Steve a grim look, and he discreetly winked back at her.

"Let's go in your office, Steve," she said. "Let's have one of the Orangeville cops listen in as a witness, too. But the other one needs to keep an eye on him!" she gestured towards Willard Dupre, who was already explaining that he was an ex-cop himself...

"This way, people," said Steve. "I want two junior editors in the room, too." He led the group down a hallway lined with photographs of former editors. The group entered his office: a large, high-ceilinged room with tall windows and dark woodwork. He gestured for all of them to sit down. "Okay, Anna. This better be good, considering the high drama."

"It is."

"Okay, then. Whatcha got?"

"I got the original election results from the Longbottom recall."

"So? Old news, Anna."

"Not hardly. These election results are the opposite of what became the public record."

"Let me see that." Steve Ballast reached for the paper that she held out to him.

"Notice that Robert Jaston won on this tally sheet!"

Steve frowned as he looked at the paper more intently. He turned to his computer and began to pull up old issues of his newspaper. After a minute, he pulled up the issue that had published the recall election results. His frown deepened as he read the election results again. He looked at the tally sheet again. Clearly, he had questions.

"Notice the official date-stamp of the Town of Longbottom on the tally sheet," interjected Anna quickly. "That authenticates the tally sheet." The two junior editors leaned forward to get a look for themselves.

"I have to ask you, Anna, where this came from. How did you happen to come by this?"

"You know I represent the Jastons, Steve. The whole Town of Longbottom knows it. I'm notorious for it. Let's just say a little birdie dropped this piece of evidence on my doorstep, without revealing who they are, to me. Am I supposed to sit on it? Of course not! I represent the Jastons to the utmost of my ability, which is why I am here, with you. I want you to go public with this piece of evidence!"

"Whoa, Anna! Do you realize what this means?" Steve asked.

"Of course. It means there was a massive election fraud!"

Petite Anna Ebert raised herself to her full height, green eyes blazing. "So, are you going to do your newspaperman's job and expose this massive election fraud? Or are you going to just go along to get along, like everybody else?"

"You never made anything easy for anyone, Anna," said Steve wryly.

Anna stood utterly still, staring him down, as he shamblingly sat down in front of his computer. He pointedly did not look at the two junior editors in the room, who were soaking up every nuance of the situation.

Steve inhaled deeply, held his breath for a long moment, then exhaled sharply. "The election fraud means that your client, Jaston, and his people, won the election, which has serious implications towards the eminent domain land grab that the Longbottom officials are trying to pull off. This is indeed a major story. I'm going to run it in our weekly local edition, and bump it up into our regional edition, too."

He nervously ran his lanky right hand through his thinning brown hair. "I just hope this story doesn't cause some of our advertisers and sponsors to drop us. But I guess we'll have to deal with it then."

"Thank you! Thank you!" exclaimed Anna Ebert. "My clients, the Jastons, thank you, too!" She smiled a huge, gleaming smile at him.

"Who is that weaselly fellow who chased you into this office?" asked one of the junior editors.

"His name is Willard Dupre, and he is, or rather, was, a client of mine. I just fired him as my client. He was trying to stop me from bringing this evidence to you."

"He's been in the main newsroom with the other cop, trying to explain that he's an ex-cop himself. As if that gives him the right to run red lights, speed, chase private citizens, interfere with newspaper business, and so on," said Steve.

"He didn't mention being an ex-cop when he came to my office," said Anna. "He told me he wanted to have a will drawn up."

"We'll have to check the record on him, see if he's legit, or if he's just a thug."

"I'm inclined to think he's just a thug, the way he tried to run me down in the street," said Anna. "I saw the evil look in his eye! I wouldn't be surprised to find out he's working for the Longbottom politicos!"

"We'll check that out, too. I'm going to need all the angles on this story. It'll probably run over the course of a few days. I'll run the opener in the Sunday edition, which has the greatest readership," said Steve.

"Wonderful!" said Anna. She turned to the Orangeville cop. "I'm done now. Arrest me if you must. I agree that I was speeding."

The cop looked embarrassed. "No need, miss. You obviously were on a mission. Not to mention you were being chased."

"That I was."

"So, in my discretion, I'll forgo the arrest, and not issue a speeding ticket, either."

"Thank you, officer. That's wonderful. Actually, I do need your help. My car got damaged in the ride over here, by Willard Dupre's truck. He rammed the back of my car and damaged the fender. Is there any way you can issue a citation to him for damaging my car?"

"We'll do you one better, miss. We'll arrest him for leaving the scene of an accident. Furthermore, he tried to prevent you from delivering a story to the newspaper, which was a violation of your constitutional rights of free speech and freedom of the press. No doubt he's tied into that story somehow, and, I suspect, not in a good way."

"Thanks again, officer."

"Don't mention it." He smiled wryly. "Just try going a little lighter on the gas pedal, so I don't hafta arrest you on your way out of town."

"Got it." Anna laughed for the first time that day, her thin face crinkling into a river of laugh-lines.

CHAPTER 42

It was the talk of Longbottom on the following Sunday morning. It was the talk of all the towns surrounding Longbottom. It was the talk of political talk radio in the greater Boston area. The telephone calls kept coming in to the radio station, as quickly as they could be answered.

No one could believe that such brazen election fraud had been carried out in Longbottom. Furthermore, no one could believe the secret of the election fraud had been successfully kept from the public for so long. People spoke of the "political machine" of Longbottom with a certain disgusted awe. The public callers speculated who the "members" might include. Everyone knew that Michael Quinn was at the center of it, even though he didn't hold any political office. Attorney Tobias Meachum was named, with references made to his father's legacy. Rufus Fishbane, the Town Clerk, was named, and seen as the most responsible party for the fraud. Then there were the three selectmen: Danny Tripiano, Gerald Hopper, and Marilyn Hardy.

Robert Jaston and his comrades were named as heroes for standing up to the machine.

"So, when's he gonna take office, as he rightfully should?" asked a curious caller to the radio station.

"Good question, caller!" said the radio commentator. "We'll have to put that question to the candidate, Mr. Jaston. I'll have my assistant put in a phone call to him. We'll see if we can get him to comment on our show!"

The talk on the radio station continued, while in the Jaston household, the telephone began to ring.

"Hello?" said a child's voice.

"Is this the Jaston household?"

"Yeah. Should I get my mom?"

"Actually, we want your father."

"He's in the barn."

"Then get your mother."

"Okay." There was a sound of the phone being laid on its side. Then, a pause.

"Mrs. Jaston speaking."

"Mrs. Jaston, this is Radio Station WROW in Boston, Political Talk Radio calling. We have a question about your husband's recent run for office of selectman."

"Oh!" There was a sharp intake of breath. "What's this all about?"

"Mrs. Jaston, have you read your Sunday morning newspaper yet?"

"No." There was a pause, then a tentative, "We're on our way to church soon."

There was a chuckle on the other end of the line. "Well, you might want to glance at the newspaper before you leave for church."

"Why? I hope there's no more trouble!"

"Actually, it's good news for you and your husband, Mrs. Jaston, "

"Really?"

"Indeed it is!"

"Oh my! It's been so long since we heard any good news, I can hardly believe it."

"Believe it! It's printed in black and white, and all over the internet."

"What's the news? I haven't brought the newspaper inside the house yet..."

"Your husband's won the recall election!"

There was silence on the telephone.

"Mrs. Jaston?"

"Is this a prank call?"

"No, it's not!" The voice on the other end was indignant.

"It better not be, because I don't have time for foolishness!"

"Go check your newspaper on your doorstep, then!"

"Okay, I will!" Once again, the phone conveyed the sound of being placed on the countertop. Then the sound of rustling pages.

"Oh my God!" screamed Maureen into the phone. "We won! We actually won! This changes everything! Thank you, thank you for the news, sir!" she continued to scream.

"Mrs. Jaston...Mrs. Jaston...when will you tell your husband?" The commentator struggled to regain control of the interview.

"Right now, this minute!" she said into the phone. Then, in an aside, she said, "Shaina, honey, run down to the barn and get your father to come up to the house this minute! Hurry! Tell him it can't wait!" Back into the phone, she said, "He'll be up to the house in a minute, if you can wait."

"That's fine. We'll come back to you. In the meantime, we'll take another caller." The phone went into a music mode in Maureen's ear.

Maureen began dancing a jig in the kitchen while keeping the telephone attached to her left ear. A huge grin was on her face. Layla was watching her from the doorway to the family room. She, too, was smiling hugely. She was relieved to see her mother happy, for once.

Robert came bursting in through the kitchen door, followed closely by Shaina. He was panting from having run up to the house.

"Take a look at this headline, Robert!" said Maureen triumphantly.

Robert picked up the newspaper. "Election Fraud Unmasked" was the headline. He began to swiftly read the article. According to the newspaper, their attorney, Anna Ebert, had made a dramatic entrance at the newspaper headquarters, where she had presented a damning piece of evidence. The evidence was a copy of the actual machine tally, which showed that Robert Jaston and his people had won handily. The results which had been announced publicly by Rufus Fishbane had been the reverse of the actual tally. The actual tally had been authenticated by a date/time stamp of the Town of Longbottom, showing the date of the election.

Robert Jaston began grinning. "Anna Ebert is a helluva lawyer."

"Isn't she?" agreed Maureen, still clamped to the phone.

"So what's going on?"

"WROW is on the line. They want to talk to you about this newspaper article, and what you're going to do."

"Are they on now?"

"It's music right now. But they'll be back on the air with us any moment."

"Okay," said Robert. "I'll take the phone."

Maureen handed it to him, planting a kiss on his wrist. Robert's jet-black eyes twinkled and his mouth curved in a smile. Maureen hadn't seen Robert look so handsome in a longtime, she realized.

Robert stood, feet athwart, head cocked at an angle, telephone held to his right ear, waiting. At last he began speaking: "Robert Jaston, here."

"Have you read the newspaper expose?" asked the commentator.

"I've skimmed it, in preparation for this phone call. I'll read it again, more thoroughly, later on."

"Tell us your thoughts."

"My thoughts? I'm thinking that I'm awfully glad this has come to light, because by winning the office of selectman, along with the others I ran with, we can reverse the vote on the eminent domain."

"I'm not following you," said the radio commentator.

"Well, it hasn't come out in the newspaper article, but underneath the election fraud was a struggle over whether my farm would be taken by eminent domain."

"How much land do you own, Mr. Jaston?"

"One hundred acres, more or less."

"Oh! I didn't realize this matter involved a

significant parcel of land."

"Darn right it does."

"Do you know what the political machine wants the land for?"

"I've heard whispers around Longbottom that they're trying for a casino."

"A casino! That's rich," the commentator began to chuckle.

"They intend to get rich off it, I'm sure," said Robert Jaston.

"No doubt," concluded the commentator. "So what'll you do, now that you've found out that you've won?"

"Take office."

"How will you do that?"

"Go up to town hall to get sworn in, I guess."

"Do you anticipate any problems?"

"Maybe."

"And then?"

"Call my attorney, Anna Ebert. She's done a pretty good job so far, don't you think?"

"She's a crackerjack," said the radio commentator. "But if you have any problems, give us a call here at WROW, and we'll follow up on the matter, okay?"

"Sure thing."

"Good luck, Mr. Jaston."

"Thanks."

The music abruptly returned, so Robert hung up the phone. He turned to Maureen and embraced her. He buried his nose in her fragrant, auburn hair.

Maureen hugged him back, grinning and giggling.

Shaina went over to her parents and wrapped her arms around them both. Layla followed her twin sister's example and hugged her parents from the opposite side.

"Jacob!" called out Maureen. "Group hug! Come join us!"

"No way," called out Jacob from the adjoining family room where he was playing a video game. "But congrats on winning, Dad! I always knew you were a winner!"

Chapter 43

Robert Jaston and his political team, including his attorney, went to town hall on a sunny, clear Monday morning, following the newspaper expose. He and his team had all dressed formally. Robert was wearing his only suit for the swearing-in ceremony at the town clerk's office.

Rufus Fishbane met them at the counter, looking like someone who was smelling rotten garbage. In fact, his complexion was tinged an unhealthy green. He tugged on his short, dark beard agitatedly. "This matter hasn't been adjudicated in a court of law," he said, poking his fingers at them in a vaguely obscene gesture. "I think it's a bit hasty to be drawing conclusions based on newspaper articles and media reports. I, for one, have to be convinced that all these articles and media accounts are accurate." He then smoothed his hands across the wooden counter of the town clerk's office, as if to say he was establishing a firm and inviolable boundary there.

"Rufus, give it up," said Anna Ebert.

He drew himself up to his greatest height, looking down his nose at them. "Counselor, I suggest that it is you who are in the wrong here."

"Rufus, don't play high and mighty with me. You know damn well that this tally sheet showing the correct outcome of the election is genuine. In fact, I think you must have played a central role in the fraud, seeing as

217

how town clerk is responsible for running the election." Her green eyes blazed with indignation as she dangled her copy of the tally sheet before him, taunting him.

"Are you making unsubstantiated accusations?"

"No, I'm proving them here and now."

"Bitch!"

The word caught them all by surprise.

Rufus had, up to this moment, always maintained a rigidly polite demeanor, even though often he was either cold as ice or hot as a boiling steam kettle.

Anna, theatrically turned to the others and said, "Now is that any way to treat a lady?" She fluttered her hand under her chin and rolled her eyes.

Her audience grinned, then swiveled their heads to look back at Rufus. His formerly greenish-tinged complexion had become nearly purplish in his rage.

"Say what you want; I am unable to swear in these three as the new selectmen, based on uncorroborated media reports." He crossed his arms across his chest.

"Rufus, hear me out," said Anna. "You will swear in these three people as the new selectmen of Longbottom or I will sue you. Personally and in your capacity as town clerk. I will seek a mandatory injunction against you, which is a court order that compels you to do the required action, in this case, swear in the new town officers. Do you understand?"

Rufus was silent but gave no indication that he had understood or that he intended to comply. Behind him, fragments of dust lazily drifted on a shaft of sunlight that came in through the tall, painted-shut windows. They were all, for a moment, frozen in time.

"So, Rufus, what'll it be?" Anna Ebert's voice cut through the silence.

He continued to stand utterly still, his head bent down, as if listening for some far-off voices to give him advice. "I'll think about it," he said at last.

"We'll give you a few minutes to collect those thoughts," said Anna. "I realize this is a strain for you..." She didn't want to lose momentum, with her political posse standing and waiting behind her.

Rufus turned away from the counter and began sorting papers from a pile to one side. He appeared to be going about his ordinary business.

"Rufus Fishbane! What the hell are you doing?" Robert Jaston exploded.

"I'm sorting the backlogged dog licenses."

"What the hell for?"

"Because I'm town clerk and this is what I do."

"And town clerks also swear in new officers."

"This is true."

"Which you are not doing."

"This is true."

"I guess you want to be sued."

"Not really."

Robert Jaston and Rufus Fishbane, both tall, lean, physically strong men, stared at each other intently, neither breaking his gaze.

"You're going to jail, Rufus. I'll make it my business to escort you there personally," Robert stated.

"Nice try, farmer boy. If anyone's going to jail, it's you for that fire you started at Quinn's house. Don't think you're off the hook for that little fiasco."

"That's bullshit and you know it," Robert retorted.

"Yeah, right!"

"Stop it, you two. You're worse than two mongrels in a dog fight! Get this straight, Rufus; I will be filing in court for a mandatory injunction against you, unless you swear them in here and now," said Anna Ebert.

"Go ahead," said Rufus. He grinned suddenly. "Make my day!"

"So you think you're Dirty Harry now?" said Robert contemptuously.

Rufus laughed, his teeth showing around his dark red tongue. He pulled at his short, dark beard in a kind of perverse defiance.

"You've got the 'dirty' part down pat," said Anna Ebert. "Come on, everyone. We've got work to do! We're going to court!"

CHAPTER 44

Once again Robert Jaston found himself dragged away from his beloved farm to have to go stand in a court of law. This time, however, Maureen was with him, and Anna Ebert was armed with the request for a mandatory injunction. A group of friends had come to support him and his political team-mates. Maureen and their friends sat in the dark wooden benches behind the railing that divided the courtroom midway.

Robert and Anna sat at the plaintiff's table, which was inside the courtroom railing, along with the rest of his political team. None of them had any small talk to utter, and thus sat in complete silence. Anna had laid out her paperwork before her, along with her physical evidence.

The current selectmen, along with town clerk, were represented by Attorney Tobias Meachum. The selectmen and Rufus Fishbane sat at the opposite table, quietly talking amongst themselves. Attorney Meachum appeared to be very confident.

"All rise," commanded the resounding voice of the bailiff. The judge suddenly swept into the courtroom, and mounted the steps to the highest seat in the courtroom, the judge's bench. The seal of the Commonwealth of Massachusetts, mounted on the paneled wall, gleamed above his head of thinning hair.

Judge Sorbett, a thin, sallow man, with an unfortunately bulbous nose, settled himself amongst his

221

black robes that he wore over his street clothes. He located his gavel and turned to the court clerk. "What's on the docket for today?" he asked.

As if he didn't know, thought Anna Ebert. As if all these newspaper reporters here in his courtroom, stuffed into the jury box, pens and tape recorders poised, are somehow just a coincidence. She resisted the impulse to smile and maintained an attentive, respectful demeanor.

Anna noticed that Steve Ballast was among the reporters placed into the jury box. She avoided making any eye contact with him.

"Good morning, Counselor," said Judge Sorbett to Attorney Meachum. "Haven't seen you out on the golf course lately..."

"Good morning, Your Honor," said Tobias Meachum to the judge. "We'll run into each other soon at the Club, no doubt, Your Honor."

Oh, so that was an open declaration of the old-boy network, was it not? thought Anna Ebert. Something I'll never, ever be a part of.

She was conscious of everyone in the courtroom staring at her as she began to present her case, but her mind concentrated on exactly what she wanted to say. She recapped all of the events leading up to her request for the mandatory injunction, mainly for the benefit of the press. She was aware of the judge looking angry. It seemed he didn't want all the sordid details aired fully, or maybe he just wanted to get off the bench and back to his golf game. Nevertheless, she persisted, even showboating slightly.

Then it was Attorney Meachum's turn. He took the

position that a proper chain of evidence had not been maintained in the instance of the election tally sheet.

That the election tally sheet could have very well been fabricated. That it was all fabricated evidence. Where was there a witness who would swear to the truth of the evidence?

Anna felt the ground slipping away beneath her. She was going to have to have something more.

Judge Sorbett turned to Anna and looked hard at her. "Counselor, do you have any witnesses who can testify to the allegations you make?" He had a slight, mean-looking smile on his face.

He's already made up his mind against me and my clients, Anna thought despairingly.

"Judge," called out a voice from the back of the courtroom.

All heads swiveled to the source of the voice. Standing up within the rows of the spectators was Clarisse Quinn. A collective gasp sounded in the courtroom.

"You're out of order! Bailiff, remove that woman from my courtroom," snapped the judge.

"Your Honor," said Anna Ebert in a ringing voice. "I call that woman, Clarisse Quinn, to the witness stand!"

"On what grounds?"

"On the grounds that she has relevant testimony to the matter at hand." Boy, do I hope she does, Anna thought. I don't want this to turn into a fiasco in front of the courtroom and all the reporters.

Judge Sorbett put his fingers around his bulbous

nose and pulled on it, thinking.

As he considered the matter, Tobias Meachum said, "Objection."

Judge Sorbett cut a quick glance over to the jury box filled with reporters and said, "Counselor, I'm inclined to hear the witness, at least for a bit." He turned to face Clarisse. "Young lady, come up to the witness box."

After Clarisse was sworn in, Anna approached her and asked her an open-ended question, something she generally avoided doing at all costs. "Tell us about your connection to the election tally sheet."

In a soft voice Clarisse began to tell the story of how she used her husband's copy of the town hall key to get into the town clerk's office and, once inside, she found the original tally sheet tucked away in the town clerk's top desk drawer. She described how she made multiple copies of the original tally sheet on the office copy machine, and then date-stamped each one with the insignia of the town clerk's office, as evidence of what she had found. She proceeded to describe how she had hidden the evidence in her kitchen, amongst her pots and pans, until she had arranged a drop to Attorney Ebert in the town library. Then she explained why she was testifying now about this matter, because she and her husband, Mickey Quinn, had had a significant disagreement.

"Thank you, Mrs. Quinn," said Anna.

Tobias Meachum sprang up. "Mrs. Quinn, what is the nature of the disagreement between you and your husband? Isn't it true that you are testifying here today out of a misguided sense of revenge?"

"I don't think it is misguided," said Clarisse Quinn. "My husband is having a child with another woman, and you know all about it, Mr. Meachum, don't you? You're the one who wrote up the paperwork about this child."

"I don't have the foggiest notion what you're talking about," said Tobias.

"Don't lie, Attorney Meachum. Don't you lawyers take some kind of oath before the court to always tell the truth?" exclaimed Clarisse.

Tobias's face was stony with anger. "I am not the party on the witness stand. You are! And I submit to the court that Mrs. Quinn is the liar!"

"Objection!" yelled out Anna Ebert. "He has no right to badger the witness this way! Furthermore, if he has been directly involved with the Quinn family affairs, he is hardly an impartial party to this whole matter!"

The gavel pounded repeatedly on the broad desk of the judge. "Counselors! Enough! I expect attorneys, at least, to respect the dignity of this court!"

Judge Sorbett cranked his head sideways to face the jury box filled with reporters who were hanging onto every salacious word. Seeing them there, he sighed heavily. He dreaded the news accounts of today's events in court. The newspapers were such rags as it was.

"Let's see the election tally sheet, Counselor," said the judge to Anna Ebert.

Silently, she handed over a copy of the evidence to him. He spent a long minute studying the date-stamp insignia on the page. He put his reading glasses on for a closer look, turning the page this way and that.

"Let the record reflect that this court finds the election tally sheet evidence to be valid, especially in light of the testimony of Clarisse Quinn."

A spontaneous 'hurray' arose from the crowd in the courtroom.

"Silence in the courtroom!" commanded the judge, banging his gavel on the desk several more times. "In light of what has transpired here today, I am hereby ordering a mandatory injunction be placed upon town clerk. He is to swear in the new selectmen forthwith!"

Rufus Fishbane made an ugly grimace in response to the judge's utterance as the courtroom erupted into excited cheers and haphazard conversations. He stood up quickly and walked out of the courtroom.

The three selectmen who had sat with Rufus Fishbane seemed dazed and slowly gathered their things to leave.

Tobias Meachum was up at the judge's bench, seemingly arguing with Judge Sorbett over his decision. The judge was explaining it all again and getting irritated with Tobias. Finally, the judge stood up to leave, and Attorney Meachum turned away. He went to find Anna Ebert, who was smiling jubilantly.

"How did you get past my judge?" murmured Tobias Meachum in her ear. There was a peculiar light in his eyes as he regarded her.

His hatchet-shaped head seemed particularly unpleasant, she thought.

"I don't know what you mean! Aren't all cases decided on their merits?" she replied in an equally soft voice. With that, she turned back to her clients and their expressions of satisfaction, vindication, joy!

"Come, sweetheart," said Robert to Maureen, putting his arm around her shoulders. "Let's go home and tell the kids we've won officially, now. In a court of law. I'm beginning to believe that this nightmare has an end."

"I've got some more work to do in this case," said Anna Ebert suddenly, giving Robert and Maureen a significant look.

"Clarisse, you mean?" whispered Maureen, raising her hand to her lips to hide her words.

"You got it. She's in mortal danger," Anna whispered back.

"What can we do?"

"Hide her. On your farm," Anna whispered.

Maureen made a conscious effort to erase the worried look from her face and replaced it with a broad smile. She slowly scanned the room and noticed Attorney Meachum watching her and Anna. Maureen turned sideways, caught Anna's arm, and whispered, "We're being watched."

"Of course."

"How does she get to us?"

"She's already on her way, with a friend. But you two need to get home, fast."

"Will do." Maureen wound her arm around Robert's and gave a gentle tug.

"Not feeling well, honey. Too much excitement for me. I need to get home, be with the kids. Can you take me there now?"

Robert nodded and they left the courtroom.

CHAPTER 45

Clarisse Quinn had descended from the witness box when she had finished testifying and quickly walked to the rear of the courtroom. She had stood against the back wall without moving, except for her eyes darting over the crowd, assessing the situation. In the moments when all eyes were fixated on Judge Sorbett as he examined the election tally sheet, Clarisse had slipped out between the heavy doors of the courtroom without a sound.

A moment or two later, Sophie Parsons had followed her out into the courthouse hallway. "Mrs. Quinn," she half-shouted.

Clarisse had been halfway down the curved, marble staircase when she heard her name called. She glanced backward and upwards, clearly frightened. She jogged down the steps even faster than before.

"I'll take you wherever you want to go, Mrs. Quinn," Sophie Parsons called down to her from the balcony. "But we have no time to lose!"

She rushed to follow Clarisse down the stairs and catch up with her.

Clarisse burst out the front door of the courthouse and ran toward the parking lot.

"Don't take your car," called out Sophie Parsons. "They'll have an alert out for your car!"

Clarisse paused in her flight to glance behind her again. "Who are you?" A gust of wind swept up her golden hair against her cheeks. "Who sent you?"

"I'm a friend of Anna Ebert's!"

At the sound of Anna's name, Clarisse relaxed slightly. "Why did you come after me?"

"Because Anna indicated that she was concerned about your safety." Sophie Parsons's big frame, wearing an open pea coat, towered over Clarisse's thin form. Clarisse looked up at her, dubiously.

"When? How did she guess I'd be unsafe?" Clarisse's blue eyes were huge with suppressed terror.

"In the days before this hearing, she and I have been talking."

"About what?"

"Like what to do to protect any witnesses that came forward. And what I should put in my next political cartoon." Sophie's curly red hair billowed out around her face as she grinned. "Come, let's keep moving, and let's go in my car. We'll talk about where I should take you on the way."

Above them a face followed their progress across the parking lot from the second story window of the courtroom.

They scrambled into Sophie's car, a used Toyota, and peeled out of the parking lot. As they pulled away, a few spectators from the courtroom crowd emerged from the courthouse. Sophie fervently hoped that everyone was too far away to have caught her license plate number.

Clarisse was staring at Sophie Parsons with fascination as they made their way away from the courthouse vicinity. "So you're the person who draws those awesome cartoons?"

"Yep. That's me!" Sophie gripped the steering wheel firmly, until her fingers were white with tension. She kept glancing in her rearview mirror. "I'm an artist, and that's my little sideline."

"You have no idea how mad those cartoons made my husband."

"I can imagine," chuckled Sophie. "Anna was taking constant shit for those cartoons. As have I."

"What kind of shit?"

"Oh, veiled threats of violence. Strange clicks and beeps on my phone, which makes me think I'm being bugged. For all I know, this car is bugged."

"Great, we can't even talk in here." Clarisse looked stricken with terror again.

"Not really."

"So where are you taking me?"

"I won't say, but you'll see for yourself soon enough."

The remainder of the car ride was utterly silent. Clarisse pressed her lips tightly together, determined to not say another word that could inadvertently reveal her whereabouts. Sophie turned on the radio to a blues station and began singing along to the song. She was only so-so, thought Clarisse, but she was clearly enjoying herself.

The Toyota chugged along the back roads of Longbottom at a moderate pace. Sophie was careful not to speed and draw attention to herself. As they got away from the thickly inhabited parts of town, and into the countryside, both Sophie and Clarisse began to breathe a bit easier.

Suddenly, Clarisse knew where she was, and she could barely restrain herself from exclaiming out loud. As they rounded the bend of the narrow country road, the Jaston farm came into view.

Sophie approached the farm as if she were going to drive past it, then abruptly turned into the curved, gravel driveway that led up to the farmhouse. She put her finger up to her lips to indicate that Clarisse shouldn't utter a word. Silently, they got out of the car and walked up to the farmhouse.

"I can't believe you brought me here," whispered Clarisse as they left the car behind.

"Where else could you go on a moment's notice in Longbottom?"

"You're right," admitted Clarisse.

"You'll hide out here for a few days, in the attic, until we figure out a plan to get you far away from here without anyone knowing."

"I can't thank you enough," said Clarisse, her eyes suddenly brimming with tears.

"Hey! You're the brave one; you had incredible guts to get up and testify in an open courtroom." Sophie reached over to give her a brief hug. "Inside with you, now!"

Clarisse stepped up on the granite doorstep and entered the Jaston farmhouse.

CHAPTER 46

"So what do we do with her, now that we're hiding her?" said Maureen to Anna Ebert.

They stood in the farmhouse kitchen, nervously looking out the warped, multi-paned window over the sink. The afternoon sun glowed a fiery orange behind the bare-fingered trees on the edge of the farm. They could both see the narrow road as it curved down past the farm's driveway. So far, no cars or trucks had come this way. Yet they were similarly apprehensive that somehow, someone had found out where Clarisse had been taken.

Maureen, with her sturdy build and auburn hair, looked much larger than tiny Anna Ebert, whose figure was narrow and straight over a mop of wiry, black hair. They bent their heads together to whisper. "How do I keep my children from accidentally revealing that we've got an unexpected guest in the house?" asked Maureen.

"I just thought of something," said Anna. "Does Clarisse still have her cell phone on her?"

"Probably..."

"We've got to get it away from her, right now, this instant. We have to throw it far away into the woods. The authorities can trace her whereabouts by tracking her cell phone!"

Maureen blanched and lurched for the stairs that led to the second floor and then up to the attic.

Anna started to bite on her index fingernail as she

re-positioned herself squarely in front of the kitchen window. She would be the look-out while Robert and Jacob were in the barn, milking the cows.

Three minutes later Anna heard Maureen rattle down the stairs. Maureen ran into the kitchen, hand outstretched with Clarisse's cell phone in it. "Here, take it away!"

"I'll leave this minute. I'll throw it out of my car, someplace far away from your farm."

"Good. Leave now!" ordered Maureen.

"I am. Bye!" Anna hurried to the kitchen door, flung it open, and ran to her car. She drove off, leaving a tall plume of dust behind her on the gravel driveway.

Maureen watched the dust slowly settle back down as it glittered in the setting sun. She hoped that no one would come by and wonder who had left in such a hurry. If asked, she would say she had no idea.

Anna drove quickly, yet carefully. She noted that there were no other vehicles on the road when she left the Jaston farm. She didn't pass any other vehicles until she had made two more turns on her route. She drove the back roads towards Orangeville, figuring the farther away the phone landed from either her house or the farm, the better.

Soon she came to a fork in the road. One road led directly to Orangeville, the other road led to a state park, with miles of open land. Anna stopped at the stop sign, pondering. A car behind her beeped, annoyed that she was taking too long. She jerked forward with her car, thereby taking the road to Orangeville. Fate had decided the matter.

She would drop the phone in the tall, uncut winter grass near to the bus station in downtown Orangeville. But first she would wipe it down, to make sure it was free of fingerprints. Once the phone was traced, the assumption would be made that Clarisse had skipped town on the earliest Greyhound bus. An alert would be put out on the bus lines for her, which would fail to yield her up to them.

***

Layla and Shaina sat cross-legged on the floor of the attic, as they listened to Clarisse tell them why she was hiding in there. The twins sat open-mouthed, eyes shining with excitement, cheeks flushed.

"Sometimes women don't choose very well when it comes to husbands," said Clarisse. "Do you girls know what I mean?"

"Not really," said Shaina, shyly. "We don't have any husbands. We don't have boyfriends, even."

"How old are you girls?" asked Clarisse. "Maybe I shouldn't be telling you any of this."

"We're ten," said Layla.

"Well, you're old enough to be sensible about boys, am I right?"

"Yes," they said in unison. Shaina tugged on her braids in anticipation.

"Well, let me tell you this: It's important not to choose the boy who's popular and handsome and funny, but mean, but instead, choose the boy who's nice, even if he's not as popular, or as handsome, or even as funny.

Niceness will get you somewhere.

"I made a bad mistake. I chose a man who is popular and handsome and funny, but he's mean, and he's not loyal to me. He started having another girlfriend, even when he was married to me." Clarisse's face quivered for a moment, but she recovered herself and went on. "I also found out that he was doing some mean things to good people who didn't deserve it." She rubbed her hand across her forehead.

"Like who?" asked Layla.

"Well," said Clarisse, "I don't know if I should tell you..."

"Tell us, tell us!"

"Promise you won't tell that I told you?"

"We promise!" they said in unison.

"The people my husband was being mean to, is being mean to, is your father and mother and you three kids. Your family. My husband is being mean to your family."

Layla and Shaina were struck silent by this sudden knowledge. They both gazed at her with new fear, of her and of what she meant to them and their family. Suddenly they weren't sure whether they should be talking to her. Their mother had not given them permission to come up to the attic.

"What's your name?" ventured Shaina.

"Clarisse Quinn." She rubbed her forehead again. "I'm getting a headache. My husband is Michael Quinn, although people call him Mickey."

Layla and Shaina looked at each other furtively. They had heard that name spoken in their house often enough, and not in a good way.

"I'm going to have to get away from him, you know," Clarisse said in a low voice. "If he finds out I'm here, he'll come here and kill me." Clarisse suddenly looked very scared as she imagined that scenario.

Neither Layla nor Shaina knew if they were safe anymore. Reflexively, they hugged one another. Their hearts pounded as they imagined a huge, angry man lunging up the stairs as he searched the house for Clarisse. They imagined him, red-faced, huge-handed, and hairy, searching under beds, inside closets, and behind doors. At last, he found Clarisse, and he began to curse her, before stabbing her, or shooting her, or both! They imagined a nasty pool of blood seeping from her fallen body, soaking into the floorboards, and the terrible mess it made. And the noise! Her screams as she died! Ah! They could hardly bear the thought of it all.

"We have to go now," said Layla in a trembling voice. She reached for her twin's hand to clutch onto, as they shakily rose from their cross-legged, seated position.

"I'm sorry, girls. I didn't mean to frighten you," said Clarisse. "It's just that I have one more very important thing to tell you both."

"What?"

"Please don't tell anyone that I'm here at your house. Not even your best friend."

"We're each other's best friend."

"Good. That's good. So you two won't tell anyone else. Right? Promise?

"Promise," they answered in unison.

CHAPTER 47

Maureen was shaking and teary-eyed. She had just listened to her twin daughters' quick-whispered account of Clarisse's ordeals and fears. Maureen was scared silly for them all. She silently prayed that no one would find out that Clarisse was at the farmhouse.

But Maureen was also fighting mad at Clarisse. Clarisse had no right to scare her daughters with talk of Mickey Quinn coming after her to murder her. As if the murder would take place at the farmhouse, in front of the girls. As if the girls would be witnesses to such brutality and horror. Her poor girls would have nightmares tonight and for nights beyond. What had Clarisse been thinking?

Maureen reached out both hands, to soothe the brow of each girl. Their foreheads both felt feverish, as if their panicky thoughts had inflamed their bodies from within.

"Girls, girls," said Maureen in a soft, slow voice. "Everything's going to be fine. Nobody knows that Mrs. Quinn is here, and we're going to have her go to an even safer place in a few days. Alright?"

"But what if that Mr. Quinn comes here, anyway?" said Layla.

"Don't worry," said Maureen. "Your daddy's got his deer-hunting rifle if he needs it to protect us, remember?"

"Oh," said Layla, who looked at her twin with

confusion and alarm.

"People don't just come inside other people's houses unless they're invited," Maureen amended quickly. "And Mr. Quinn is definitely not invited."

"So he can't come inside and find Mrs. Quinn?"

"No, he cannot. We'll never let him inside."

The corners of Layla's mouth eased into relaxation. Her eyes sought Shaina's: what was she thinking? Shaina was busy fiddling with her socks, pulling them up her legs and folding them over at the knee. Layla wondered if maybe she was being too much of a scaredy-cat. She decided to believe her mother that everything would be okay.

***

Maureen climbed the attic's narrow pull-down ladder in her stocking feet, so as to not make any noise. She carried a small flashlight in her right hand that slightly impeded her climbing. As her head poked up, Maureen shone the flashlight around the attic. She spotted Clarisse lying across the mattress on the floor, apparently asleep. The sheets Maureen had provided her with were barely tucked in around the edges.

She sleeps the sleep of the innocent, thought Maureen. Only, this time, it's the sleep of the guilty. Because Clarisse has scared the wits out of my girls, thought Maureen sourly.

Clarisse was breathing evenly, one arm flung upwards, in a gesture emblematic of haste, of thoughtlessness, of defiance.

238

Maureen began to nudge Clarisse with her big toe. Maureen's flexible feet were clad only in socks, and she wriggled her toe deeper between Clarisse's ribs.

Clarisse rolled away, onto her left side. The annoying foot followed her. She opened one eye in the darkness, found the beam of light from the flashlight, and stared directly into it. "Maureen," she breathed. "Thank God it's you!" She yawned hugely. "What's going on?"

"What's going on," said Maureen in a harsh whisper, "is that you've scared the living daylights out of my two girls, and I don't like it one bit. Just what the hell were you thinking? That kind of talk simply cannot go on around here, do you understand?"

"Oh," said Clarisse, in a little voice, realizing that she had made her all-powerful, all-necessary protector angry with her. She blinked repeatedly, wishing she could blink away the reality of what she had just done.

I'm such a fool, she thought to herself. I've gotten myself into a fix simply because I got involved, because I cared, because I was angry at my husband. Now here I am, laying on a mattress on the floor of a farmhouse attic, scared for my life, simply because I've been hopelessly idealistic. And I've run my mouth to two ten-year-olds, like the thoughtless fool that I am. I really am an idiot, she thought.

Her mouth drooped, as if she was about to bawl.

"I know you didn't mean to scare them on purpose," said Maureen, relenting slightly. "But you've got to promise me that that won't ever happen again, and that you won't come down the ladder again, even to use the bathroom, except in the middle of the night. We gave you that old chamber pot with the lid to use for when you're stuck in the attic. We'll keep it clean for you, even though it's a nasty job."

"I hate using that thing. I feel guilty that you have to clean it," said Clarisse. "But getting back to the girls...You know I didn't talk to the girls down in the main house. They came up to see me, in the attic. But I shouldn't have spoken freely, that's for sure. I'm very sorry. Can you accept my apology?"

"Yeah, I guess so." Maureen drew in a sharp breath. "But meanwhile, we'll have to work on getting you out of here, and on your way as soon as possible. And I owe you an apology, too. I've been yelling at you when I haven't said a proper thank you to you for your brave testimony. It was your testimony that won the mandatory injunction for us, which is going to set everything right. You are an incredibly brave woman."

Clarisse felt a sliver of warmth creep back into her heart after her bout of silent self-chastisement. "Thanks. I don't know about being incredibly brave, but I'm incredibly bored up here. Could I have a book or two, with a lantern or a flashlight?"

"Sure," said Maureen, who smiled at Clarisse for the first time since she had come up to the attic. "I'll bring up something juicy."

"Thanks," said Clarisse. "I don't mean to be demanding..."

"Don't worry, you are, but it's okay. Okay?"

"Yeah. But can I shower downstairs, in the middle of the night?"

240

Always pushing the envelope, thought Maureen. She heaved a sigh. "I suppose. You can, after everyone's gone to bed. But I only want you to use a flashlight in the bathroom, understood? Don't turn on the light, which could be seen from outside the house at night. Do you agree to those terms?"

"Absolutely. You have my word on it," said Clarisse.

CHAPTER 48

The hunt for Clarisse was on. Mickey Quinn had duly reported his wife to be missing to the Longbottom police.

The first reaction of the local officer taking the phone call had been incredulity. Did Mickey Quinn really expect that his wife would return home after she had just finished testifying against him and his cronies? Was it any wonder that she had gone missing? Unless the tricky bastard had done her in himself. Which was not out of the question. Not by a long shot.

But, for now, the Longbottom police department was taking the position that Mickey Quinn was not a murderer, and that his wife, Clarisse, had genuinely gone missing. A series of initial calls were put out to all probable leads, including her out-of-town family and friends. A trace was put on her cell phone signal. The police department was not surprised that she had apparently ditched her phone in the vicinity of the Greyhound bus station.

However, they were rather taken aback when, Clarisse's cell phone began to move from one location to another. The police were not amused when they discovered that a homeless man had found the cell phone and put it in his pocket, thereby carrying it around downtown Orangeville. The homeless man was indignant when the police relieved him of the cell phone.

"Finders, keepers!" he shouted at the police. "Possession is nine-tenths of the law!" he added.

"That one has spent time with jailhouse lawyers, sounds like," said one cop.

"If he keeps it up, he'll be spending more time with 'em," said the other officer.

The initial search for Clarisse yielded no results, which left Mickey both angry and unsettled. Not only did he have a seething, blood-pressure-popping desire to see Clarisse stone-cold dead, but he found himself in the uncomfortable position of being an undeclared suspect. He was officially a person of interest, whatever the hell that meant, he grumbled to himself. He was being looked at as a 'suspicious character' by regular folks in Longbottom, who ordinarily never dared to look at him cock-eyed. In fact, most of the older men used to doff their caps to him before all this.

Now he was an item to be examined, like a bug under the microscope. Life wasn't quite as grand as before, he admitted to himself. Well, they couldn't indict him for her murder. For one thing, they weren't even sure if she was dead. No dead body had showed up anywhere. And, for another, he hadn't killed her. Though he sure felt like killing her. They couldn't indict him for mere wishful thinking, thank God. The cops weren't mind-readers. At least not yet.

Mickey looked around his barroom for a friendly face from his seat in the corner booth. Everyone in there was turned away from him, not making eye contact. He began to count customers. His place seemed emptier than usual. He hoped he and his place weren't the target of an unspoken boycott in town, just because of Clarisse's disappearance.

He raised his handsome face towards the ceiling, with a bemused smile, eyes half-lidded. He would maintain outward confidence, no matter what. He stretched his arms akimbo, hands clasped behind his head as he leaned way back in his seat. He yawned elaborately. After a long minute, he rose to march into his office.

He was grateful for the solitude the office provided him. He was safe from prying eyes. He decided to spend the evening going over his tallies from earlier in the week.

Time crept slowly, as he checked the clock every half hour or so. Finally it was closing time. A knock on his door made him sit up straighter behind his desk. "Come in," he said.

As the door swung open, Mickey saw that it was Darlene. Her front-side was beginning to pop forward, but at this point, she just looked like she had put on weight. Her sharp edges have softened, thought Mickey.

"How are you feeling these days?" he asked.

"Well, I probably won't barf on your shoes again. I seem to be past most of my morning sickness."

"Let's hear it for an absence of barfing!" He winked.

Darlene rolled her eyes. "Here's the receipts and also the cash and credit slips from tonight. I'll be seeing ya." She turned on her heel to go.

"Darlene..."

Her hand was already clasping the doorknob. She

sighed heavily. "What?"

"What are people saying about me?" Mickey asked, an urgency in his tone. "You hear 'em talking out there on the floor...What are they saying?"

Darlene cast her head to one side, pondering whether to say anything at all.

In a quiet voice, she said, "People don't know what to think, exactly. The town's divided. Half think you did her in and spirited her away. The other half thinks she ran away, and you had nothing to do with her disappearance." She shook her head, to clarify. "Well, they think she ran away after she went against you in court. Because she's afraid of you. So, in that sense, you did cause her to flee. But that half doesn't think you killed her." Darlene began to blush. "I'm sorry if I'm speaking too candidly."

"Not at all," he answered quietly. "And you?"

"What about me?"

"What do you think I did?"

Darlene absentmindedly began to rub her belly in a comforting way while she thought some more. "I don't know what to think," she mumbled.

The silence between them stretched into a long moment. Darlene raised her head to look at him directly and found him staring at her. His eyes, normally sky-blue, were nearly black in the dim office light. She couldn't read his expression. She felt a shiver travel up her backside, up into her neck.

"Do I seem like a killer to you?" he asked softly.

"I, I don't know."

He smiled slightly. He pulled out the right-hand

drawer of his desk, lowered his right hand into the drawer, and drew out something she couldn't see.

Darlene shrank backwards.

It was a key. A small key. She didn't recognize its kind.

"As you can see, it wasn't a gun." He smirked. "As if I would shoot the woman who is bearing my child."

"What kind of key is that?" asked Darlene, vastly relieved, and feeling a sudden urge to pee. She ignored the urge, knowing she couldn't flee at this exact moment.

"It's a safety deposit key, from a bank. From Longbottom Savings Bank, in fact."

"Oh."

"Do you want to know why I brought it out now?"

"Umm. I guess so."

"To show you where the key is, in case something happens to me."

"Like what?"

"Jail, or some other inconvenience."

Darlene looked at him funny.

"Not that I killed her. I didn't. It's just that if they don't find her soon, the authorities may decide they need a fall guy. And it just may be me."

"So what would I ever do with the key?" asked Darlene.

"Get money for yourself and the baby."

"Oh."

"So now do I seem like a cold-blooded killer to you?" he asked.

Darlene wiped her upper lip of sweat. "I guess not."

"Thank you for your vote of confidence."

"You're welcome. Can I go home now? I'm kinda tired."

"Soon. I just have another question or two for you."

"What?"

"Do you think we could ever raise the child together, somehow? So I would be able to see and know my own child?"

"I doubt it," said Darlene. "I can't imagine how that would ever work out."

"Well, you and the baby could live with me in my big house, now that Clarisse is gone."

"You seem awfully sure that she's gone," said Darlene, suspicion tingeing her voice again.

"Oh, I'm sure, alright. She's scared witless after what she pulled in court."

"No, I'm fine in my little apartment. Thank you."

His eyes, black in the shadows, looked down at the key in the palm of his hand. "Okay. That'll do for now. You can go." He placed the key back in the drawer.

"Thanks. I've gotta use the john before I go home." Darlene ran to the ladies room, making it just in time. Strange bird that Mickey Quinn is, she thought afterwards, as she washed and dried her hands. Having his child was the devil's bargain. If she had known things would have turned out this way, would she still have gone forward with the pregnancy?

Well, it was too late now. She was in her fifth month, going into her sixth. Far too late to change her mind. She dreaded to think that there was a possibility that Mickey was a killer. She involuntarily shuddered.

What an awful legacy for her unborn child. Heaven help them all!

CHAPTER 49

Mickey Quinn reached for his cell phone and dialed.

"Yep?"

"You awake?"

"I am now. What the hell? It's three a.m.!"

"I got something for you."

"Now?"

"Tomorrow night, this time."

"You couldn't wait 'til morning?"

"No."

A prolonged sigh threaded through the phone. "Okay." Another sigh, followed by a groan and a yawn. "What is it?"

"I wanna do the farmer's place. Wipe it off the land, once and for all," Mickey told him.

"Jesus! Are you sure?"

"I'm sure."

"It ain't gonna be easy. Especially in twenty-four hours."

"Forty-eight, max."

There was a pause on the other end. "Alright. But I want the money up front, cash."

"How much?"

"Hundred-thou."

It was Quinn's turn to groan. "Half before, half afterwards."

"What am I? A sucker? Once it's done, I won't be hangin' round to collect the other half..."

249

"Ever heard of the postal service? UPS? I'll get it to ya somehow..."

"Bullshit! Get me the whole thing or forget it!

"You seem to forget who works for whom around here," said Quinn.

"Who works for whom!"...mimicked the falsetto phone voice. "That last thing you had me on, chasing that lady lawyer, almost put me in the slammer!"

"You deserved it. You botched that one, big time!"

"Look, do you want me or not?"

"I do."

"Just get me the money, and we'll get on with it..."

"Come by my office tomorrow evening, and I'll have the money."

***

Mickey swiveled his chair to face the wall behind his desk. A huge, black-and-white photo of a sailing ship hung there, contrasting the wood-paneling. He lifted off the photo, revealing a built-in safe. He fingered the combination lock until it sprang open.

Inside were stacks of money, bundled and tied. He began counting the piles of bills to see how much was there. He reached ninety thousand. Shit. He was a little short.

Plus he didn't want to completely empty his safe. He needed a minimum of ten grand in there for emergency expenses. He'd have to take ten grand out of his bank account to make up the difference. Considering how things were looking these days, that would be looked upon as a suspicious move. Damn. Well, then again, he could say he needed the cash to hire a lawyer. Everybody would understand that. He smiled. Yep, the lawyer excuse would do.

***

Mickey strode into the Longbottom Savings Bank, head held high against the sly stares and whisperings that sprang up as he passed clusters of people. He went up to the inquiry desk and asked to see Denton Clay.

"Down the hallway, second door on the left," replied the bank clerk.

He rapped twice on the door, hard, then opened it without waiting for an answer. Denton was on the phone, his left hand twirling locks of his wispy white hair into formations of devil's horns. He was concentrating on his phone call and didn't see Quinn right away. Upon noticing him, Denton blanched. He ended the phone call as soon as possible.

"Hello, Denton."

"Hi, Mr. Quinn." His voice quavered. "What brings you here today?"

"I want to take out a cashier's check , and I'd like you to do it personally, since I don't want word of it getting out."

"How much money are you talking about?"

"Ten thousand."

Denton blinked. "I trust that everything's on the up-and-up."

"Of course."

"May I ask what will it be used for?"

"A lawyer I'm hiring for my defense, not that it's any of your god-damned business"

"Ah."

"So, can we get on with it?"

"Of course. Follow me." They walked out to the bank lobby. Denton ducked behind the bank counter and snatched a form. He turned on the automated machine that printed out the cashier's checks. "Who do I make the check out to?"

"Willard Dupre."

Denton smoothed his expression and kept his eyes downcast. "Here you are, Mr. Quinn."

"Thanks, pal."

"You're welcome, Mr. Quinn."

"See ya." Mickey slipped the cashier's check into his wallet, flicked his eyes about to see who else was there. Satisfied, he strode out the door to the parking lot.

Everything was going according to plan.

***

Denton scurried back to his office. He reached deep into his desk drawer for the town phone book. He looked up a phone number and wrote it down on a slip of paper.

Of course, he could have looked up the phone number on his computer, but he also knew that computers always left a trail. This had to be done without a trail.

He left the bank on his lunch hour. He stopped at a

local convenience store run by newly-immigrant Indians. He wandered about the harshly-lit aisles, picking out a pretzel snack and a six-pack of beer. He paid, then wandered out to the parking lot where his car was parked. He tossed his purchases in the back seat of his car. He had parked as close as he could to the lone pay-phone booth attached to the side of the building. Shards of broken glass glittered against the blacktop pavement and strands of crab grass grew in the cracks. Graffiti defaced the side of the phone booth. Cigarette butts, stomped flat, spilled the tobacco and filters in a windswept bunch at his feet. Denton Clay huddled against the phone booth, his back to the street. He slid the slip of paper out of his pocket and dialed the number.

"Hello?"

"Mrs. Jaston?"

"Yes..."

"I'm a friend. You don't know me. You and your family are in danger, big danger, starting right now, a man named Willard Dupre, a known thug, hired by Mickey Quinn, is coming after you and your family, tonight!"

"How do you know this?"

The even sound of the hang-up-dial-tone met Maureen's ear.

Denton wiped his face of the thin layer of sweat. He shoved the slip of paper back in his suit-pants pocket. A light wind whipped his white wispy hair into a halo around his head. He felt deeply anxious, yet also relieved. He had acted on the side of angels. He only hoped his action would be enough to stem the onslaught of violence and rage that was surely coming the Jastons' way.

CHAPTER 50

Maureen Jaston trembled fiercely. The phone call she had listened to a moment ago had left her almost speechless with fear. She swiveled her head to the window, half-expecting to see an ominous vehicle, a looming truck, or an anonymous van come creeping up the road and park itself alongside their farm. She stared hard, and saw there was nothing there now, in the middle of the day. Of course there wouldn't be. They would come at night. She had today, only today, to prepare her family to protect itself. And to protect Clarisse, she remembered a moment later.

Jacob and the twin girls would be home from school in about another three hours.

Everyone would have to be ready to hunker down, or escape. She and Robert would have to decide. Oh, God. She needed to tell Robert this minute.

Outside, the drizzle had tapered off, leaving a silvery film on the shaggy grass. Maureen pulled on her mud boots over her red socks with the hole in the left toe. She managed to mend everyone's clothes but her own. Maureen darted out of the kitchen door, sliding on the granite doorstep, which was slick with rain. She nearly toppled, then righted herself. She sprang off the stone onto the tall grass, running full tilt towards the barn. "Robert!" she screamed.

Robert's lean form poked around the corner of the open barn door. "Maureen? What is it, honey? Are the kids alright?"

Maureen charged at him, running into his opened arms. She panted, "I just got the scariest phone call, ever!" She tilted her head back to look deep into his opaque, black eyes. "They're coming for us! Tonight!"

"Who?" he said. "How do you know?"

"I told you already," she babbled, "I got a phone call from someone, someone who wouldn't say who they were, but who also said we're gonna get it from Mickey Quinn and a henchman of his called Dupre."

"Dupre? Billy Dupre?"

"Yeah, "

"Fuck! This is serious. Dupre is bad news."

"How bad?"

"He's part of the Boston Irish Mob, even though his name is French. Don't ask me how or why, I don't know. I gotta get you and the kids outta here!"

"We're not going without you."

"I'm not leaving, but you and the kids are. I'm not leaving a hundred head of milking cows here unattended and unprotected, it'd be a mass slaughter!"

"We're not leaving without you," repeated Maureen, her tone rising.

"You and the kids are not staying! You can't!"

"We're not leaving!" shouted Maureen. "If we leave, they've won! If we stay, they have to kill all of us, one by one, to get our land! If we leave you alone, they only have to kill you, because we've already abandoned the land! Don't you see?"

As if in answer to her furious, convoluted logic, the bare-branched trees near the barn shivered and hissed their agreement, despite an absence of wind. Maureen's cheeks were aflame, and her auburn hair floated diagonally about her shoulders. She waited as Robert considered her words.

"You'd put your children's lives on the line for this farm?"

"Our children. Your children, too. And yes, I would, for this family's farm."

"Sometimes survival is more important than the land."

"Sometimes survival is sticking to the land, rather than fleeing. What good is being chased away? Being chased from place to place?"

"You still have your life in the end."

"At the cost of your dignity, and your freedom!"

"Freedom? Dignity? Or is it pride?" Robert's black eyes glittered. "They say pride goeth before a fall..."

"Robert, are you telling us all to bail?" She shook her head violently. "I don't believe it! You're not the brave man I thought I married!"

Sudden tears sprang to her eyes. She sniffed. When she spoke again, her voice was strained. "I guess you're all talk! All talk about the unity of family, about sticking together through thick and thin, about how this farm has to stay in the family, no matter what!" She waved her arms wildly, in frustration. "You're gonna go down like the Lone Ranger, with no witnesses, even, and me and the kids will be off somewhere else, where we don't even want to be..."

"Alright, alright, alright," said Robert Jaston exasperatedly. "You and the kids can stay. Just stay the hell out of the way of any bad guys that come around, you hear?" He ran his fingers through his shaggy salt-and-pepper hair and swallowed hard.

"I'll probably end up dead in the end, it'll happen over my dead body, just like I predicted, way back in the beginning."

"Not if I have anything to do with it," vowed Maureen.

Chapter 51

Willard Dupre planned his crimes methodically. For this upcoming one, he went about filling each gas can at a different gas station, so as to not arouse suspicion, then stashed it under the tarp stretched out in the bed of his dusty, black truck.

As he drove around Longbottom, he eyed the townspeople surreptitiously from his rearview mirror. Idiots, he thought. They have no idea what it's all about. These suckers slave their lives away on no account jobs, for what? To sit in some retirement home, playing bingo, when they're all wrinkled and too feeble to do jack shit?

Me, I'm outta here after this one. Maybe I'll hit Bermuda or the Caicos, or even Belize. Gonna drink big drinks with little umbrellas. Check out the local womenfolk. He smiled broadly at the thought.

Four gas cans later, he headed for home. Home was an apartment atop a motorcycle shop that was known to be a haven for local drug dealers. The Longbottom cops knew, or purportedly knew, of the non-motorcycle business, but let it be. Willard Dupre, called Billy Doper by some, was its protector from the local cops, or so it was said.

Willard parked his truck behind the motorcycle shop. The building stood alone on the state highway, surrounded by deep forest. No would would bother, or even see, his truck behind the shop. He locked his truck, secured the tarp over the gas cans with more bungee cords, and glanced all around. Satisfied that no one was near, he shoved his keys into his jeans pocket, and mounted the wooden stairs to his apartment.

Unlocking his door, he instinctively checked for signs of intruders. All seemed intact. He relaxed a smidgen. He proceeded to pace through every room of his apartment, checking to see if anything was amiss. Only when he had satisfied himself that all was truly untampered with, did he relax.

He cooked himself a bachelor's breakfast for his late lunch: fried eggs, bacon, with melted cheese, all layered on toast. As he bit the sandwich, the runny egg-yolk dripped onto his wrist, which he licked off. He washed it down with a tall glass of orange juice. His hunger satisfied, he belched. His dirty plate and dirty frying pan went onto the pile in the sink to be dealt with later.

Later, later. He meandered towards his unmade bed, and sat on its edge to take off his jeans, shirt, and shoes. Mostly undressed, but for his socks and underwear, he laid back onto his bed. He intended to take a long, day-time nap. He needed to be fresh for the night's work ahead.

***

Willard awoke abruptly at sunset. Remembering what he was about to do that night, he felt a jolt of electric pleasure. He grinned to himself, revealing small, yellowed teeth. With his tilted eyes and long, thin nose, he looked like a human version of a fox. His fox-like appearance was heightened when he donned dark jeans, a black T-shirt, and a thick, black hoodie that accentuated his sinewy build. He began humming a tuneless song with pleased anticipation.

"Rags," he said aloud to himself. "I need rags." He went to his narrow hall closet and drew out a half-dozen, bleached-out, ripped towels. He began tearing them into halves and thirds, dropping them into a pile at his feet. When he was done, he carried the entire bundle over to his kitchen table.

"A bucket," he muttered to himself. He didn't have any in his apartment. There would be plenty of spare buckets in the motorcycle shop below. They wouldn't miss just one. Quietly, he opened the door from his apartment, and looked all around from his vantage point at the top of the wooden landing. Seeing no one, he descended the stairs and tried the back door of the shop. Locked. Of course. After hours, the shop was closed. He could make a trip to the local hardware store, but he didn't feel like it. He might be noticed and commented upon. He wanted to stay out of public view, and possible public opinions.

He eyed the outside of the shop. Along its back wall, there were three plastic five-gallon buckets with plastic-and-wire handles, all lurid orange, lined up against the building. One was filled with bricks. The second was filled with rusty metal parts. The third was filled with sand and cigarette butts. He considered making quick work of it, dumping the sand and cigarettes, but that would be noticed immediately in the morning.

Sighing, he unloaded and stacked the old bricks one by one, until he could claim that bucket. Glancing about once more, he took the bucket back up to his apartment. Inside, he stuffed the bucket with the pile of rags; it was overfull. Later, he would transfer the bucket to the bed of his truck.

All he needed to do now was wait for the appointed hour.

CHAPTER 52

The moon tangled in the bare tree branches at the top of the hill, riding low. Just as well, thought Willard Dupre. I won't have to use a flashlight to go about my business. He parked his truck around the bend from the Jaston Farm, off the road, almost into the underbrush.

He walked around to the bed of his truck and climbed in. He took some of the rags out of the bucket and stuffed them into a black garbage bag. The remaining rags he left in the bucket and began to pour gasoline over them, soaking the rags. He filled the bucket with more gasoline than he needed, figuring he would use it on the remaining rags later.

This damn bucket is heavy, he thought to himself as he strained to carry it along the road and onto the Jaston's gravel driveway without sloshing it over the edge. He was carrying it in almost complete darkness now, as the moon had disappeared behind some clouds.

As the farmhouse came into view, he saw that a light burned alongside the front doorway, and another alongside the kitchen door. The rest of the house seemed to be dark. Willard Dupre grinned to himself. Should be easy, he thought. And if he ran into any trouble, he had his trusty gun stashed in its holster under his jacket, just where he needed it.

"Go after his livelihood," Mickey Quinn had instructed him. "Not only do I want the farmer and his family off the land, I want the farm itself erased from the land, you understand?"

Willard had mock-saluted him.

Now he approached the barn on the side away from the house. Tired, he put the bucket on the ground at his feet. The gasoline stank, making his head swim. He reached into the bucket and pulled out the first rag, hating that his hand was now also soaked in the gasoline.

The rag was cold and slimy in the night air. He flung it down at the foot of the barn. He reached into his jeans pocket for his cigarette lighter, and squatted to light the rag. The flame shot up, huge and blue. It illuminated the stone foundation of the barn and the angular, tall autumn-crisp grasses. The grasses burst into orange relief, then flamed out. The rag burned futilely against the foundation of fitted field stones. Looking closer, he saw the foundation went about four feet high in the back of the barn. He reached for another rag to stuff into the crevice between the field stone foundation and the beginning of the wooden structure. He lit the second rag, which flamed hugely for a moment, then died out against the density of the massive timbers which made up the walls of the barn.

Frustrated, Willard Dupre walked around the barn to his right, closer to the side of the farmhouse. As he did so, an automated light, mounted on the barn's outer wall, sprang into high beam, showing him and his bucket in stark relief. He crouched into a defensive position, waiting to be attacked. He braced himself for a dog to leap onto him. When nothing came after a long minute, he stood up and began to laugh softly. This farmer really was unprepared to defend himself, he thought. He doesn't even have a dog to guard his farm. He walked around to the back of the barn, where he had tried before, to try again. He began to stuff another rag between the field-stone foundation and the timber walls. He'd get this damn barn burning if it was the last thing he'd do, he muttered to himself.

***

In the middle of the night, Clarisse had used the ladder to climb down from the attic, while gripping the flashlight in her teeth. She desperately had to use the bathroom, and she refused, on principle, to use the antique chamber pot that Maureen had brought up for her.

Clarisse crept along the second floor landing, taking care to not make any noise. She found the bathroom, pushed open the door, and, per instructions, shut off her flashlight. As she washed her hands afterwards, her gaze wandered out the window to the drooping moon and the pinpoint stars. As she looked, she saw lights alongside the barn flash on, and the outline of a man running. "Here comes trouble," she said.

Grabbing the flashlight, turning it on, Clarisse burst into the master bedroom down the hall. She shined the flashlight towards the bed, and saw a rumple of sheets and quilts. "Someone's out by the barn!" Clarisse said in a low, urgent voice. "It's an emergency. Hurry."

Maureen sat up in bed, fully awake. "Robert's downstairs with his rifle. He must have fallen asleep."

The two women ran down the stairs, not bothering to remain quiet, despite the sleeping children. Maureen was first into the front room. Robert was indeed fast asleep, fully dressed, in a sitting position on the easy chair nearest the front door, with the rifle propped across his knees.

Maureen motioned for Clarisse to hang back. Maureen, herself, was careful to approach Robert from the side away from the muzzle of the gun. "Robert, honey," she said gently, reaching out a hand to stroke his rumpled hair. "Wake up, honey."

With a jerk of his head, Robert opened his eyes and gripped his rifle harder. "What's happening?"

"There's someone lurking outside the barn," said Maureen. "We don't know what they're up to yet."

Robert stood up. "Where are they?"

"Hold on, honey, not so fast."

"I'm gonna get whoever's after my farm!" Robert said.

"Honey, what about some backup? Shouldn't we call 911?"

"I don't trust 'em. Half of 'em are in with Mickey Quinn. The other half are too scared to stand up to him, like when they came to arrest me..."

Clarisse was staring out the window. "I see flames," she announced.

"Where?" said Robert and Maureen in unison.

"At the barn," said Clarisse.

"That's it, I'm shooting that no good S.O.B.!" Robert burst out the front door of the farmhouse, rifle in hand, and ran down the path towards the barn.

***

Willard had heard voices at the distant farmhouse door when it opened, and knew he had but moments to accomplish his goal and get away from the scene. The barn was proving to be a tough customer to burn down. This old-time barn, built with the massive, dense, wooden beams, had become almost iron-like in strength. The flames would burn the gasoline residue on the rags, plus the rags themselves, but then just smoke on the surface of the wooden beams. This damn barn needs a bomb, thought Willard. He stuffed yet one more gasoline-soaked rag in the crevasse between stone and beam and held up his cigarette lighter.

"Put that lighter down, asshole," said Robert Jaston, pointing the rifle at him.

Billy Dupre dropped the lighter to the ground, reached inside his jacket to his holster, and in one fluid motion, pulled out a pistol and shot two shots at Robert Jaston.

Robert felt a stinging in his left arm and thigh. Knowing he was hit, he lifted his rifle and shot back. The side of Billy Dupre's face disappeared, and his body slowly slid to the ground and lay in a crumpled heap.

Robert Jaston closed his eyes and stood there, motionless. He began to cry, silently, knowing his life was as good as over, from this moment forward.

***

Maureen and Clarisse stood at the farmhouse front window, holding hands, listening. They heard the two shots from the pistol, followed by the deep roar of the rifle shot.

"Oh my God, I hope he's not dead," moaned Maureen.

"He's not," said Clarisse. "Robert shot second, he's still alive."

"I'm going down there, to see what happened," said Maureen.

"I'm coming, too," said Clarisse.

Maureen didn't bother to tell her to go back into the attic to hide; everything was too far gone and, anyway, she was glad of the company.

Hand in hand, the two women ran down to the barn. They continued around the back side of the barn where they met Robert standing alone, standing vigil over the crumpled form at his feet, weeping.

"Robert! You're okay!" exclaimed Maureen joyfully.

"No, I'm not. I'm hit. And I killed a man."

"Where are you hit?"

"Somewhere in my arm and also my leg, on my left side."

"Come back to the house with us," commanded Maureen. "We'll call an ambulance for you."

"And the cops...for dead Billy Dupre..."

"That scum," said Maureen. "Good riddance."

Robert leaned on Maureen and handed off his rifle to Clarisse. "This time I'm really gonna go to jail for killing a man."

"Nah, it'll work out somehow," said Maureen. "Anna Ebert will figure out a way. In the meantime, we need to get you inside, to see how badly you're bleeding."

***

Mickey Quinn had been unable to stay away from the skullduggery planned for the middle of the night. He had an itch to see Billy Dupre at work; Billy had attained a certain level that he knew he couldn't match. For one thing, he didn't walk as far outside the law as Billy did. Second, he was really looking forward to seeing the barn go up in flames. He could anticipate the smell of burning cow flesh, a mighty waste of steak, as far as he was concerned.

Knowing that Billy was scheduled to arrive at 3:00 am, Mickey had planned to show up a bit afterwards. He had parked Clarisse's Subaru behind Willard's truck. The bend in the road was the perfect place to conceal the vehicles from the farm. He began walking up the asphalt road by moonlight that alternately slipped behind the clouds.

As he fully rounded the bend, Mickey saw the small, shadowy figure of a man juxtaposed the immense side of the barn in the moonlight. Then he saw the motion detector lights flash onto Willard, throwing his presence into stark relief.

Mickey decided to stay well back in the shadows, under the cover of a huge oak tree, where the moonlight did not penetrate. He watched Willard squat to light the fire at the foot of the barn. Again. And again. Billy was having some kind of trouble. Nothing is as easy as it seems, said Mickey to himself. Not even lighting a match to gasoline.

What had surprised Mickey was the shoot-out. He had never figured that the farmer Jaston could, and would, blow half a man's head off his shoulders. Somehow that didn't square with Mickey's view of Robert Jaston. He had always thought of Jaston as one of those "back to the earth" pacifist types, who would fold if enough pressure was brought to bear.

But what shocked Mickey even more was Clarisse running out of the farmhouse, hand-in-hand with Maureen.

"So that's where the bitch has been hiding out. Figures." Without any further thought, Mickey began following the trio as they slowly made their way up to the farmhouse.

***

Jacob, Layla, and Shaina had all woken to the sounds of gunfire. Jacob sat up directly, then threw off the covers and began to get dressed. Layla and Shaina had woken, looked at one another, clutched hands, and, not saying a word, run to their parents' bedroom. They were both deeply scared to not find their parents in their bed. "Where are they?" whined Layla.

"Go back in your bedroom, you two," said Jacob, emerging from his bedroom, fully dressed. "Never mind where they are now. They're busy!"

"No!" said Shaina. "We want to see what's going on, too."

"It's too dangerous," he commanded with teenage authority. "You two need to stay out of sight. Go back in your bedroom and lock the door."

The twins shrank back in fear and withdrew behind the door of their room. Jacob hovered at the mid-landing of the stairs to the first floor. He peered down, wishing he could see around corners. He held his breath. so as to listen to the voices muffled in the front room.

"...The ambulance..."

"...the doctor...too much blood..."

Suddenly, he heard the front door to the farmhouse wrench wide open.

"Mickey!" a woman screamed.

"Hello, babe," said Mickey with a sardonic tone. He quickly scanned the room and noted the rifle resting against the tall, oak sideboard. It was beyond the immediate grasp of all three of them.

"What are you doing here?" said Clarisse, beginning to edge towards the rifle.

"Get away from the rifle, or I'll shoot you dead right here and now," said Mickey, pulling a gun from his pocket. "I shoulda known you'd hole up with the likes of the Jastons."

"You're not fit to eat the cow dung on this dairy farm!"

Mickey rolled his eyes. "Shut up bitch. You've already talked too much. I'll deal with you soon enough."

"What do you want with us?" asked Maureen,

271

trying her best to keep a pleading tone out of her voice.

"I shoulda thought that'd be clear by now, but you people are thick, aren't you? In case you didn't understand, I want you and your farm outta here, offa this land, and outta Longbottom! Got it?"

"But why? What'd we ever do to you?" asked Maureen.

"You haven't done anything, except stay in my way. I'm gonna site a casino here, come hell or high water. I'm gonna be wicked rich, and I'm gonna leave a legacy behind."

"For who?" said Clarisse abruptly.

"For my child that's on the way. No thanks to you."

"If you can believe that woman's telling the truth," said Clarisse. "She's nothing but a brainless pothead."

"Shut up. You're nothing but a gold-digger."

"Not true," said Clarisse indignantly.

"And a traitor..."

"To you and your stupid schemes?"

Mickey turned the gun to point it at Clarisse. "I'm about one second away from blowing your brains out," he glanced at Robert Jaston, "but I guess I leave that kinda thing to this guy here. That was some shot you took on Billy Dupre."

Robert didn't answer.

"You're bleeding like a stuck pig. I guess if we wait long enough, you'll conveniently bleed to death, making everything easier for everyone."

In the distance, sirens sounded.

"Shit!" said Mickey. "Who called the cops?"

The two Jastons and Clarisse looked at one another,

mutely, then in sudden, mutual understanding.

"Figures. One of the Jaston brats did it. I shoulda known." He raised his arm holding the gun and slowly began to aim it each of them, in turn. Maureen shuddered as the gun was pointed at her. Robert didn't notice, as he was concentrating on staunching the blood from his leg wound. Clarisse looked him straight in the eye, as if daring him to fire at her.

He pointed the gun at Clarisse for an extended moment.

"Look out!" screamed Maureen an instant before the gun fired at Clarisse.

Clarisse jerked backward in her armchair.

Robert Jaston sprang up from where he was sitting and tackled Mickey to the floor. Quinn still clutched to his gun in his right hand. Jacob burst from hiding on the stair landing to pile onto Mickey and wrest the gun away from him.

A sudden pounding on the front door overcame the tumult between the three men.

"Open up! Police!" commanded a voice on the front doorstep.

Maureen ran to fling open the door. "Thank God you're here."

Three cops leapt inside, quickly scanning the scene.

"Okay, son, you can get off of Mr. Quinn now," said the oldest of three cops, a red-haired fellow with drinker's burst-veins in nose and cheeks. "We'll handle it."

"Hey, Fergie, glad it was you who answered the call," said Mickey, sitting up, dusting off his arms and shoulders, as if it were perfectly natural to be found on someone else's floor, in mortal combat.

"Mickey, Mickey, Mickey," said Fergie, with obvious regret. "Whadya mean by coming down to the Jaston farm here in the middle of the night?"

"He's here for murder!" blurted out Maureen. "My husband's and his wife's."

Fergie and the other two cops swiveled to look at Clarisse, who had slumped in her armchair, a blooming rose of blood in the center of her chest. Her head rested on her right shoulder. Her face was a pale ivory, framed by disheveled blonde hair.

"Somebody check and see if she's still got a pulse," said Fergie. The two younger cops both stepped forward and knelt at her sides.

"If you wanna talk about murder, why dontcha check out Billy Dupre, back behind the barn, with his brains blown out, courtesy of the good farmer Jaston here," said Mickey.

Fergie looked askance at Robert Jaston, then back at his fellow officers.

"'Afraid she's gone, Sarge," said one of the younger cops.

"Guess we got our work cut out for us," said Fergie, sighing deeply.

"Officers! Arrest Mickey Quinn! He's the one who just murdered that woman sitting there in the chair!" shouted Maureen.

"The bitch deserved it," murmured Mickey Quinn, as one young cop undid the belted handcuffs and clicked them onto his wrists. The finality of the click seemed to have brought Mickey Quinn back to his senses, because he quickly said, "Hey, Fergie, it's me! You can't be serious about arresting me..."

"Sorry, Mickey, you crossed the line. There ain't much I can do for you, this time. Headquarters don't look kindly on stiffs turning up. Especially when the stiffs are wives or former wives. It ain't politically correct these days."

"Shit, Fergie, you're an ungrateful bastard, after all I've done for you, "

"Take him in, now," said Fergie. "We'll call an ambulance for you, Jaston. Hang on, and don't bleed out on us," he commanded. "Got any rags? Gotta bind up those bleedin' holes as tight as we can in the meantime."

After a long interval, the siren of an ambulance was heard in the distance. Maureen began to feel a bit of relief. The medical people were here, and soon he'd be in the hospital.

"You kids are coming with us," announced Maureen to the twins faces peering around the corner of the stairs landing. "I don't feel safe leaving you alone here, Jacob, to guard the farm and your sisters. Hurry! Go get dressed!"

"Officer Ferguson, will you put a police detail on our farm while we go to the hospital? I don't feel safe leaving our livestock unattended. I imagine you can see why!"

"Yes, ma'am, I do. And that won't be a problem. We'll be on the premises, checking out the murdered Billy Dupre. No one will be coming here to do any mischief, I can tell you."

CHAPTER 53

Robert Jaston woke ready to rise and milk the cows. When he made the first move to get up from bed, he discovered he was bandaged, attached to the bed with various fluid lines, and, moreover, in pain. He fell back into the softness of the bed, as he remembered he was in the hospital.

He stretched his neck to peer around the curtain that encircled his bed and saw Maureen slumped crookedly in a hospital chair. All the craziness came rushing back into his memory. He had a sudden vision of Billy Dupre's head being partially blown apart like a crushed melon. He felt leadenly sick, felt his stomach curling to bottom. His life was changed forever. No matter that it was in defense of life and land. Defense of land was no defense, he'd heard. Only defense of life mattered, and even that could be tricky. He'd be needing Anna Ebert yet again. He sighed so deeply that he began coughing.

Maureen woke, bleary-eyed. She rubbed her eyelids hard, as if she could make her sleepiness disappear. "You're awake! Thank goodness! How are you feeling, sweetie?"

"Like a sponge riddled full of holes," said Robert, feeling sorry for himself.

"Don't exaggerate, dear. It isn't attractive, and it doesn't help you heal. We need you healed, asap," said Maureen.

Suddenly worried, Robert asked, "Who's minding

the farm?"

"Jacob, the girls, and I have gone back twice a day, for two days now, to do the milkings, and other chores."

"Two days have passed?"

Maureen gave him a sharp look. "You've slept since coming out of your surgery two days ago. As if you could sleep away all of this like a bad dream."

A sheepish look passed over Robert's face. He looked down and fingered his hospital robe. "Where are the kids?"

"They're coming. I hear them now. They were just down the hall in the waiting room."

Robert looked up as his three children filed into his hospital room. "Hi, kids. It's good to see you all."

"How're you doing, Dad?" said Jacob in his uneven, teenaged voice.

"I've been better."

"You're finally awake, Daddy!" said Shaina, holding hands with Layla.

"Yes. I was very, very tired. But I'm better now." He looked at the circle of his family's faces around him. "What's it been like, going back to the farm?"

"We've had a police escort each time, which has been crucial for the girls. They've been terrified of going back," said Maureen.

"Where've you been staying the last two days?"

"Here at the hospital. By your bedside, in chairs, and in the waiting room down the hall. It hasn't been easy. We're all exhausted."

"Why? Why haven't you stayed back at the farm, since you've got that police escort?"

"We can't. It's closed off. It's the scene of a crime," said Maureen.

"Then why haven't you checked a motel down the highway?" asked Robert. "You all deserve a good night's sleep."

"To be honest, the kids haven't wanted to leave you alone here at the hospital," said Maureen. "I can hardly tear them away from here to go do the milking and other chores. They're all afraid something bad will happen to you if they let you out of their sight."

Robert's black eyes filled with grateful tears, and his face softened. "You are all the best family that any man could hope for." He wiped one cheek with the back of his hand, thereby pulling an IV line taut. He looked at each member of his family, one by one. "Listen to me: I don't want you to worry or to be afraid. Billy Dupre is dead. I killed him myself. And Mickey Quinn is on his way to jail, to be locked up behind bars for many, many years. So they won't be coming after me anymore."

"But there might be others, Dad," said Jacob, speaking for all of them.

"They'll be too scared to do anything," said Robert. "Not with the cops and everybody watching their every move. This thing has blown wide open, now."

"I guess so," said Jacob, somewhat mollified.

"I know so," said Robert. "Promise me you won't live your lives being afraid of shadows and memories. There comes a time when each of us, including me, has to make up our mind to be brave. That time is now."

"Your father is right," said Maureen. "Although," she said with a chuckle, "it's easy for you to say when you've just slept for two days. We're too tired to be brave. We haven't slept more than half an hour in the last forty-eight hours."

"You all need to get some rest. Now," commanded Robert. "Go check into the motel."

A cell phone song sounded. Maureen scrabbled in her purse for her phone and pulled it out just in time to answer it. "Hello?" she said. "Anna! What's up?"

Maureen listened carefully. Robert and their children watched her intently. A huge grin began to cross her face. "Thanks so much, Anna! Yes, I'll tell them. Thanks a million. You are the greatest, you absolutely are!" She hung up.

Turning to Robert and their children, Maureen said, "I've got some great news, everyone!" She grinned triumphantly. "The newly elected board of selectmen, who were only sworn into office yesterday, after all this went down, have just voted to reverse the eminent domain order against our house and farm!" She tossed her headful of auburn hair back over her shoulders, and added, "It was their first piece of business as the newly constituted board." She raised both arms above her head in a gesture of victory.

"Hallelujah!" said Robert, grinning hugely. "I thought we'd never make it to the finish line. But, we've won!"

"Free and clear," said Maureen. "Our land is once again ours. And all it took was a few stray gunshot wounds to my dear husband to earn it." She reached for Robert's hand to give it a squeeze. "That was too near a thing for my taste."

Maureen added. "And the police aren't pressing charges against you, Robert, because you acted in self-defense; he shot first."

"I spoke rashly when I said they'd get my land over my dead body," said Robert. "They almost did." He made a face. "Be careful what you say, it might come true."

"And what do you say now, Daddy?" asked Layla.

"I'd say I'm lucky to have my family around me. I'm lucky to be alive." His black eyes sparkled. "I am indeed a blessed man."

BOOK CLUB DISCUSSION TOPICS:

1. What do you think of the U.S. Supreme Court's decision to expand the scope of eminent domain in the <u>Kelo</u> case? Is it more important to protect individual land rights? Or is it more important to let development proceed in order to generate more tax revenue for a city or town?

2. Compare and contrast the marriage of Robert and Maureen Jaston to the marriage of Michael (Mickey) and Clarisse Quinn.

3. Why do you think that Mickey Quinn is so fixated on having a child? Do you think that the child that Darlene conceived is his? Why or why not?

4. Was Clarisse justified in informing on her husband's election maneuvers? Should family loyalty be more important than what it legally right?

5. How important are election officials to election integrity? How can the citizenry ensure election integrity? Discuss recent elections in your own community.

6. Does your community have a "recall" provision? Has it ever been used in your community? Was it used successfully or not?

7. Have you ever met a lawyer like Anna Ebert? How effective is she as an attorney?

8. How good are the newspapers, radio, TV, cable, and/or internet news sources in your area? Do they cover the political and legal news fairly?

9. Discuss your own personal involvement with local political issues. What issues caused you, or members of your family, to become involved? Did you have success in achieving your goals?

10. Discuss the writing style of *Eminent Crimes: A Legal Thriller*. What are its shortcomings? What are its strengths?